THE DINOSAUR ALMANAC

By Q. L. Pearce

This Book Belongs To

Mrs. Connie Townsend

Illustrated by Linda Bild

Lowell House Juvenile
Los Angeles

Contemporary Books
Chicago

To Julian Avi Bradford Hill
— Q.L.P.

To my Dad, who knew I could accomplish anything,
and to Bob, who continues to encourage me to do so.
—L.B.

Acknowledgments
With special thanks to Kenneth Carpenter for his invaluable advice and guidance as the manuscript took shape and to Carolyn Wendt for her patient editorial direction.

Reviewed and endorsed by Kenneth Carpenter, Chief Preparator and Dinosaur Paleontologist at the Denver Museum of Natural History.

Publisher: Jack Artenstein
Editor-in-Chief: Lisa Melton
Project Editor: Carolyn Wendt
Director of Publishing Services: Mary D. Aarons
Design: Lisa-Theresa Lenthall and Susan H. Hartman

Manufactured in the United States of America

ISBN: 1-56565-175-8
Library of Congress Catalog Card Number: 94-5359

10 9 8 7 6 5 4 3 2 1

TABLE OF CONTENTS

Introduction: Earthshakers...Tyrant Kings...Remarkable Reptiles! 4

PART I
The Ancient, Mysterious World of the Dinosaurs...5

PART II
The Saurischians.....................................17

CHAPTER 1
Running Reptiles: The Ceratosaurs, Ornithomimosaurs, and Oviraptorosaurs..........20

CHAPTER 2
Deadly Dinosaurs: The Deinonychosaurs 29

CHAPTER 3
Lords of the Mesozoic: The Carnosaurs..............35

CHAPTER 4
Early Dinosaurs: The Prosauropods 42

CHAPTER 5
Gentle Giants: The Sauropods...........................49

PART III
The Ornithischians..58

CHAPTER 6
Plates and Spikes: The Stegosaurs 59

CHAPTER 7
Dinosaur Diversity: The Ornithopoda and the Pachycephalosauria 65

CHAPTER 8
Amazing Armor: The Ankylosaurs......................75

CHAPTER 9
Horns and Frills: The Ceratopsians.....................81

PART IV
The Final Act: The End of the Dinosaurs 89

Index..95

EARTHSHAKERS...
TYRANT KINGS...
REMARKABLE REPTILES!

Saltasaurus

The dinosaurs have been called by many names. Some are deserved, and some are not. The word *dinosaur* means "terrible lizard" in Greek. Although some dinosaurs were certainly terribly fierce predators, many were gentle plant-eaters. Dinosaurs, however, were *not* lizards. They were a very diverse group of animals that lived from about 230 million years ago to about 65 million years ago.

Dinosaurs belonged to a unique group of animals called archosaurs. The archosaurs include prehistoric, flying pterosaurs, as well as the ancestors of modern crocodiles. Some scientists think that archosaurs belonged to the reptile class. Others believe that the archosaurs were special enough to be a class by themselves.

In the following pages you will learn about many dinosaurs, the world in which they lived, and the other creatures that shared their world. To make it easier to study dinosaurs, scientists have organized them into two main groups, with each group then broken down into smaller subdivisions. In this book we will profile the dinosaurs by group. But first, let's set the stage by taking a look at that time in Earth's history known as the Mesozoic Era—the Age of the Dinosaurs.

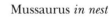

Mussaurus *in nest*

Allosaurus

4

PART I:
THE ANCIENT, MYSTERIOUS WORLD OF THE DINOSAURS

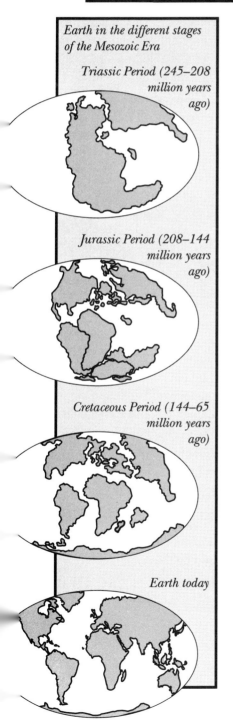

Earth in the different stages of the Mesozoic Era

Triassic Period (245–208 million years ago)

Jurassic Period (208–144 million years ago)

Cretaceous Period (144–65 million years ago)

Earth today

If you could go back in a time machine to the moment when the first dinosaurs walked the earth, you would find that our planet was a very different place. The Mesozoic, or "middle," Era, began about 245 million years ago. Way back then, all of the land on our planet was joined in one huge supercontinent called Pangaea, which means "all earth." The shores of this great continent were washed by a tremendous ocean called Panthalassa, or "all sea." But the Earth was changing. Slowly, over millions and millions of years, Pangaea split apart to form the continents we are familiar with today.

GEOLOGICAL TIME CHART

Era	Period	Epoch	Millions of Years Ago
Cenozoic	Quaternary	Holocene (Recent)	0.01
		Pleistocene	1.6
	Tertiary	Pliocene	5.3
		Miocene	23.7
		Oligocene	34
		Eocene	57.8
		Paleocene	65
Mesozoic	**Cretaceous**		**144**
	Jurassic		**208**
	Triassic		**245**
Paleozoic	Permian		286
	Carboniferous	Pennsylvanian	320
		Mississippian	360
	Devonian		408
	Silurian		438
	Ordovician		505
	Cambrian		570
Pre-Cambrian	Proterozoic Eon		2500
	Archean Eon		4600

THE MESOZOIC ERA

Scientists have divided the Mesozoic Era into three different intervals, called periods. Each period had a different climate, plants, and dinosaurs.

A Triassic landscape: The first dinosaurs, like this Coelophysis, *appeared during this time.*

THE TRIASSIC PERIOD (245 to 208 million years ago) was the first period of the Mesozoic Era. The climate was hot and dry in most places, and it changed little with the seasons. Huge tree ferns grew in the wetlands near the oceans and inland seas. Tall conifers similar to modern pine trees grew in drier areas, and there were huge inland deserts that spread over thousands of miles. About 227 million years ago, the first dinosaurs, such as *Herrerasaurus*, appeared.

Giant dinosaurs, such as this Apatosaurus, *lived in the warm, semi-dry climate of the Jurassic Period.*

THE JURASSIC PERIOD (208 to 144 million years ago) was the second period of the Mesozoic Era. The climate was warm and fairly dry. Tree ferns and palmlike plants called cycads extended along the coasts and far inland. The Jurassic Period was the age of huge dinosaurs, such as *Apatosaurus.*

The mighty Tyrannosaurus rex *lived amidst the flowering forests of the Cretaceous Period.*

THE CRETACEOUS PERIOD (144 to 65 million years ago) was the final period of the Mesozoic Era. Shallow seas covered much of the Earth. The first flowering plants appeared, and there were forests of trees that resembled oak and hickory. Many spectacular dinosaurs lived during the Cretaceous Period, including horned and armored dinosaurs and the great *Tyrannosaurus rex.*

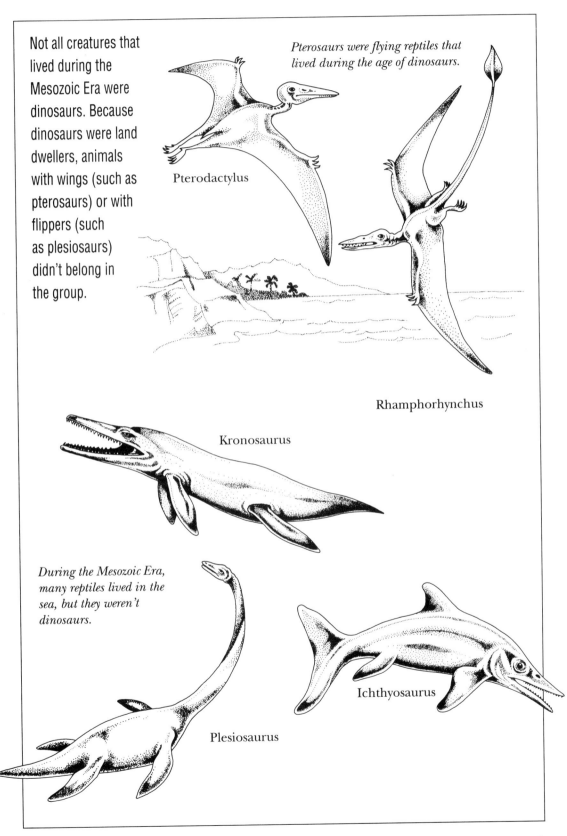

Not all creatures that lived during the Mesozoic Era were dinosaurs. Because dinosaurs were land dwellers, animals with wings (such as pterosaurs) or with flippers (such as plesiosaurs) didn't belong in the group.

Pterosaurs were flying reptiles that lived during the age of dinosaurs.

Pterodactylus

Rhamphorhynchus

Kronosaurus

During the Mesozoic Era, many reptiles lived in the sea, but they weren't dinosaurs.

Ichthyosaurus

Plesiosaurus

DO IT YOURSELF!
FOSSIL FUN

You can make your own cast of an animal's bone or shell by following these simple steps.

You Will Need
• an object to cast, such as a chicken bone or clam shell
• plaster of Paris
• modeling clay
• one or two 4 x 12-inch (10.2 x 30.5-centimeter) strips of thin cardboard
• masking tape
• newspaper
• a coffee can
• an old spoon

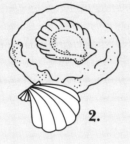

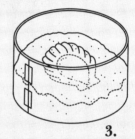

1. Cover a flat working surface with several sheets of newspaper.

2. Roll the modeling clay into a ball, then pat it down into a flattened circle that's a little larger than the object that you have. Press the back of the bone or shell into the clay to make a deep impression, then remove the bone or shell.

3. Wrap the strip of thin cardboard around the edge of the clay and tape the ends securely. (If you need to, use two strips of cardboard to completely surround the clay.)

4. Using the old spoon to stir, prepare the plaster of Paris in the coffee can according to directions, then pour it into the clay mold you prepared.

5. Let the plaster dry for about three hours, then remove the paper ring and clay to reveal your fossil cast.

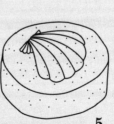

FOSSILS: KEYS TO THE PAST

The scientists who study dinosaurs are called paleontologists, and the way they learn about these amazing creatures and their ancient world is by studying fossils. Fossils are the remains of plants and animals that died long ago. When a living thing dies, it usually rots, or decomposes. Before long, nothing is left of it. In the case of an animal, scavengers may feed on the remains, leaving behind only bones. Then, decomposers —bacteria, for example—break down what is left. If given enough time, even bones and shells may crumble to bits.

Fossils, such as this Diplodocus *hind limb bone, help paleontologists better understand the world of dinosaurs.*

However, when an animal is quickly buried after death, perhaps by a landslide or a flood, the decomposers do not get a chance to do their work. The soft parts of the creature decompose, but the mud or sand surrounding the remains may harden into rock, sealing the hard parts (such as shells, bones, or teeth) inside.

KID FINDS

Scientists aren't the only fossil finders. Children have been responsible for several important fossil discoveries, too!

In 1802 in Massachusetts, a 12-year-old boy named Pliny Moody uncovered gigantic, birdlike tracks while he was helping to plow a field. The tracks seemed to be etched in stone. Because dinosaurs hadn't been heard of yet, most people thought the footprints were those of a giant bird. Years later they were identified as dinosaur tracks.

The world's first ichthyosaur fossils recognized as those of a new species were discovered in 1810 by a 12-year-old British girl named Mary Anning. Mary didn't lose her knack when she grew up. Years later she discovered the first remains of a plesiosaur.

More recently, 10-year-old Colin McEwan of Virginia made an amazing discovery while on a school field trip. While he and his friends were climbing on a pile of dirt left behind by workmen, Colin noticed a strange rock. It turned out to be the vertebrae of a plesiosaur. Colin's find is now part of the collection at the Smithsonian Institution in Washington, D.C.

Over millions of years, the remains may be uncovered by earth movements and by erosion from wind and rain. Fossils help scientists to learn such things as the size of the animal when it was alive. Fossil teeth can help scientists determine whether the animal ate meat or plants.

CREATION OF A FOSSIL

An *Elasmosaurus* dies.

Its skeleton is buried under layers of sediment, which then harden into rock. The sea creature's bones become fossilized over time.

Millions of years later, rocks are eroded away and the fossil is exposed.

TYPES OF FOSSILS AND FOSSILIZATION

PERMINERALIZATION: Mineral-bearing water seeps through the bone and slowly deposits minerals in the holes and cavities inside the bone. The original bone is still there, but it is locked up inside the minerals.

Homeosaurus *bone*

CAST: Water percolating through the surrounding rock dissolves the object completely, leaving an empty mold. The mold then fills with minerals that form a duplicate of the exterior of the object (bone, tooth, or shell, for example).

Mesolimus

STEINKERN: Mud or sand fills the empty shell of an organism (such as the shell of a sea snail) and hardens. The shell then dissolves away, leaving a mold.

Ammonites

12

CARBONIZATION: The tissues of the organism (usually plants or soft-bodied sea creatures) change to a thin film of carbon within the rock.

Seed fern

MUMMY: Remains that have dried out. Remnants of skin may be present in mummies.

Moa claw

AMBER: Ancient hardened tree sap. Insects were sometimes trapped in the sticky sap, becoming encased and preserved in amber.

Dolomedes

> **DINO FACT**
> Animals leave behind traces of more than just body parts. "Trace" fossils are such things as fossilized footprints and animal droppings.

MAIN TYPES OF FOSSIL-BEARING ROCK

Type	Description
limestone	whitish to light gray; fine-grained texture
sandstone	white, gray, tan, or reddish; sand grains visible
shale	brown, black, or gray-green; layers with fine texture

WHAT ARE INDEX FOSSILS?

Index fossils, or zone fossils, are particularly helpful to scientists. They are the fossil remains of certain groups of living things that existed for relatively short periods of time (only a few million years). The creatures preserved as index fossils were also very common during their time, and lived over a wide area. These factors make the fossils easy to identify.

The first step is for scientists to figure out the age of the fossils. Then, the next time a group of the same kind of index fossils is discovered, the find can be an important clue to the age of the surrounding rock layer, even if the rock layer has been all jumbled up by earth movements. It also helps scientists to determine the age of any other less common fossils that are within that layer.

THE DINOSAUR GROUPS

To make living things easier to understand, scientists have organized plants and animals (and those organisms somewhere in between) into groups with similar characteristics. The largest group is called a kingdom. The groups then become smaller, starting with phylum and continuing down through class, order, family, and genus to the smallest main group, species. The further

DINOSAUR EGGS

Like modern reptiles, most dinosaurs probably laid eggs, but only a small variety of fossil eggs have been discovered. Here are a few:

Dinosaur	Length of Adult	Egg Size and Shape	Location Found
Hypselosaurus	40 feet (12.4 meters)	10 inches; round (25.4 centimeters)	France
Orodromeus	10 feet (3.1 meters)	6 inches; oblong (15.2 centimeters)	Montana (U.S.A.)
Maiasaura	25 feet (7.8 meters)	8 inches; oval (20.3 centimeters)	Montana (U.S.A.)
Protoceratops	6 feet (1.9 meters)	6 to 8 inches; oblong (15.2 to 20.3 centimeters)	Mongolia

Protoceratops (*above*)
and nest of Protoceratops *eggs*

down the line you go, the more characteristics the group members have in common. Sometimes there are groups in between, such as suborders and infraorders. These groups allow scientists to be as precise as possible when trying to fit a particular creature into a group.

Dinosaurs belong to the animal kingdom, and to the phylum Chordata, which includes animals with backbones. Many scientists believe that dinosaurs and other archosaurs are a subclass that is part of the large class Reptilia, along with snakes and lizards. Some paleontologists, however, feel that archosaurs should be a separate class called Archosauria.

Once we reach the group level of order, the dinosaur group begins to be divided into smaller groups. Some dinosaurs had bony frills on top of their heads. Others were enormous in size. But the most important trait scientists use to distinguish different kinds of dinosaurs from each other isn't as obvious as frills or large size. Rather, it's the arrangement of the dinosaur's three hip-bones—the ilium (IL-ee-um), ischium (ISS-kee-um), and pubis (PYOO-biss). You might be surprised to discover that the giant plant-eater

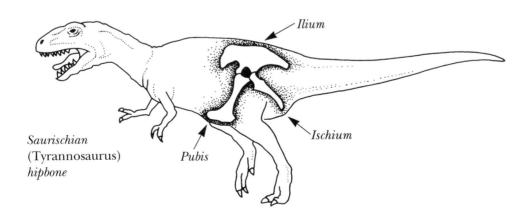

Ilium

Ischium

Saurischian
(Tyrannosaurus)
hipbone

Pubis

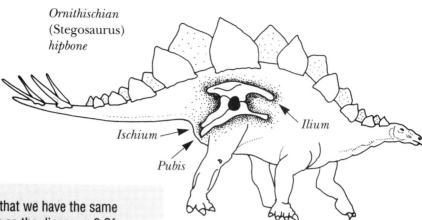

Ornithischian
(Stegosaurus)
hipbone

Ischium

Pubis

Ilium

Did you know that we have the same three hipbones as the dinosaurs? Of course, the size and structure are different, but they serve a similar purpose—to help support our body weight and to allow us to move our legs freely.

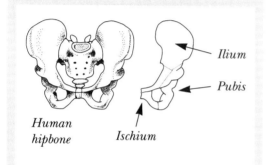

Human
hipbone

Ischium

Ilium

Pubis

Apatosaurus was more closely related to fierce *Tyrannosaurus rex* than to many other plant-eaters. Why? Because of the arrangement of its hipbones.

There were two main groups, or orders, of dinosaurs—the saurischians (sor-ISS-kee-unz) and the ornithischians (or-nuh-THISS-kee-unz). In the next two sections of the book, we will take a closer look at these two groups of dinosaurs and at the traits that set them apart from each other.

THE SEARCH GOES ON

Over the past two hundred years, the remains of many remarkable dinosaurs have been discovered. And the search is certainly not over. In 1993, two new dinosaurs were named. The fossils of *Monolophosaurus* (mahn-oh-lohf-oh-SOR-uss), or "one-crested lizard," and *Sinraptor* (SINE-rap-tor), or "China raptor," were discovered in China. These dinosaurs were both capable predators of the Jurassic Period.

Monolophosaurus *skull*

In size and shape, *Monolophosaurus* was similar to its close relative, *Allosaurus*. It's likely that *Sinraptor* resembled the slightly smaller, but equally fierce *Megalosaurus*.

PART II:
THE SAURISCHIANS

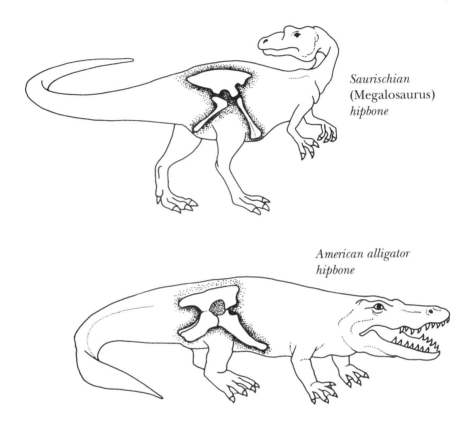

Saurischian (Megalosaurus) *hipbone*

American alligator hipbone

The saurischians are known as the lizard-hipped dinosaurs because the arrangement of their hipbones was similar to that of modern lizards. The pubis bone pointed forward, while the ischium pointed backward. *Apatosaurus* and *Tyrannosaurus* are just two of the animals that belonged to this group.

The lizard-hipped dinosaur group is divided into two smaller groups, or suborders: the Theropoda (ther-OP-uh-duh) and the Sauropodomorpha (sor-uh-pohd-uh-MORF-uh).

The Theropoda were the meat-eating members of the saurischian dinosaur group. Theropods, whose name means "beast-footed," moved on their two hind legs. Most of them had clawed, birdlike feet with three forward-pointing toes and a small, backward-pointing dewclaw. In general, they had long tails, which they held out straight as they ran. While

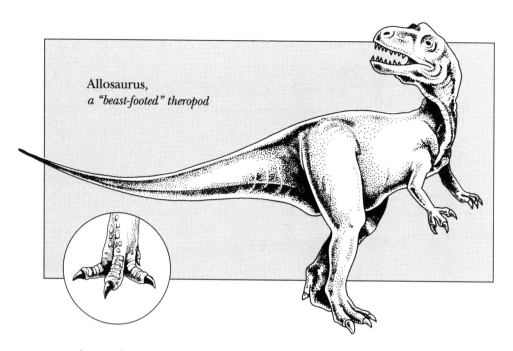

Allosaurus,
a "beast-footed" theropod

some theropods were very big and powerful, others were small and fierce. The theropods may be divided into at least five smaller groups, called infraorders.

Infraorder	Description	Example
Ceratosauria	robust, long skull	*Ceratosaurus*
	lightly built, slender limbs	*Coelophysis*
Ornithomimosauria	lightly built, long forelimbs	*Ornithomimus*
Oviraptorosauria	lightly built, deep skull	*Oviraptor*
Deinonychosauria	medium weight, ripping toe claw	*Deinonychus*
Carnosauria	large and heavy	*Tyrannosaurus*
		Allosaurus

The plant-eating dinosaurs in the saurischian dinosaur group make up the suborder Sauropodomorpha. The name *sauropodomorph* means "lizard-footed form." These dinosaurs ranged in size from about 8 feet (2.5 meters) in length to supergiants more than 100 feet (31 meters) long! Most of the large members of this group walked on all fours, but some of the smaller sauropodomorphs moved from place to place on two feet. In general, they had long tails and necks, but small heads. The sauropodomorphs are usually divided into two infraorders.

Infraorder	Description	Example
Prosauropoda	small to medium-sized,	*Plateosaurus*
	with fairly long necks	
Sauropoda	heavy, long-necked giants	*Apatosaurus*
		Camarasaurus

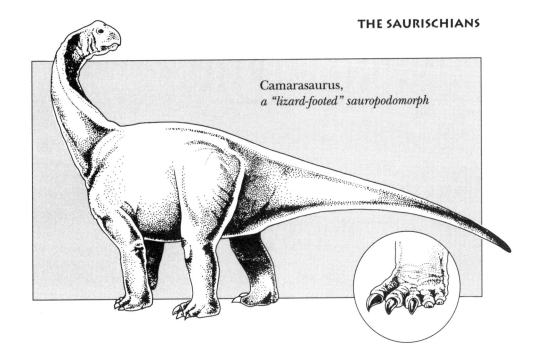

Camarasaurus,
a "lizard-footed" sauropodomorph

It's important to note that the groups we have outlined here are general. Not all paleontologists agree about how many smaller dinosaur groups there should be, and some dinosaurs don't fit easily into any particular group. However, as new fossils are discovered and studied, the relationships often become clearer.

It's also important to remember that some dinosaurs are known from only a few fossils, so some of the drawings in this book include a little guesswork about how the animals looked when they were alive.

THE LIZARD-HIPPED DINOSAUR FAMILY TREE

Order	Suborder	Infraorder
Saurischia	Theropoda	Ceratosauria Ornithomimosauria Oviraptorosauria Deinonychosauria Carnosauria
	Sauropodomorpha	Prosauropoda Sauropoda

CHAPTER 1

RUNNING REPTILES

The Ceratosaurs, Ornithomimosaurs, and Oviraptorosaurs

Until fairly recently, the ceratosaurs (sayr-AT-oh-sorz), ornithomimosaurs (or-nith-oh-MY-mih-sorz), and oviraptorosaurs (oh-vih-RAP-tor-uh-sorz) were often grouped together in a large infraorder known as the coelurosaurs (see-LOOR-oh-sorz). The differences between them finally convinced scientists that each group deserved to be in an infraorder of its own. When the individual dinosaurs were classified, however, some small theropods didn't fit easily into any of the three groups, and there is still some question about exactly where they belong.

The ceratosaurs are a newly assigned group that included some rather large meat-eaters as well as some of the earliest known theropods. These "horned lizards" were named for the stubby horns on the skulls of some members of this group. The larger animals had rather long skulls and necks, sharp, flesh-shearing teeth, and sturdy, powerful legs. The smaller creatures were lightly built and speedy, and they were generally equipped with a mouthful of small, sharp teeth.

The ornithomimosaurs didn't have any teeth at all. Instead, they sported tough, horny beaks that could easily crush tiny prey or break open an egg. With their long, slender legs and large eyes, it's likely that the ornithomimosaurs, or "bird-mimic lizards," looked a little like featherless ostriches.

The oviraptorosaurs were lightly built theropods of the Late Cretaceous Period. They had long, slender hind legs, grasping hands, and short, deep skulls that ended in toothless beaks. Oviraptorosaur means "egg-stealing lizard."

DISCOVERIES

Type of dinosaur and the modern name of the country in which it was found

CERATOSAURUS
• United States (in the Morrison Formation, in Colorado and Utah)

COELOPHYSIS
• United States (in the Chinle Formation at Ghost Ranch, New Mexico, and in the Petrified Forest National Park, in Arizona)

STRUTHIOMIMUS
• Canada (in the Judith River Formation and the Horseshoe Canyon Formation, in Alberta)

ORNITHOMIMUS
• United States (in the Denver Formation, in Colorado, and in the Kaiparowits Formation, in Utah)

GALLIMIMUS
• Mongolia (in the Nemegt Formation, in Omnogov)

OVIRAPTOR
• Mongolia (in the Nemegt Formation and the Djadochta Formation, in Omnogov)

PROCOMPSOGNATHUS
• Germany (in Mittlerer Stübensandstein in the state of Baden-Württemburg)

COMPSOGNATHUS
• Germany (in Öber Solnhofen Plattenkalk, in the state of Bavaria)
• France (in the Lithographic Limestone, in the Department of Var)

SALTOPUS
• Scotland (in the Lossiemouth Sandstone Formation, in the region of Grampian)

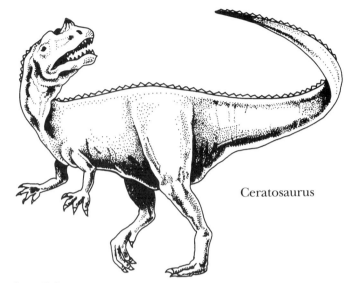

Ceratosaurus

CERATOSAURUS (sayr-AT-oh-sor-uss)

fossil skull of
Ceratosaurus

At no more than 20 feet (6.2 meters) in length, *Ceratosaurus* may not have been the largest of the Jurassic predators, but it was a powerful hunter. The ceratosaur infraorder shares its name with this "horned lizard," which had a horn on its snout. This stubby horn might have been used to battle rivals, or it might simply have provided a way for individuals to recognize each other. *Ceratosaurus* also had bony ridges over its eyes and a short, bumpy ridge that ran along its back from its neck to its tail. *Ceratosaurus* had four clawed fingers on each hand.

COELOPHYSIS (seel-oh-FY-siss)

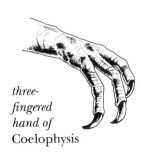

three-
fingered
hand of
Coelophysis

This Late Triassic dinosaur is one of the earliest theropods known to have lived in North America. At about 10 feet (3.1 meters) long, it was a fairly small ceratosaur—that measurement includes its very long and slender tail. It was lightly built and probably weighed no more than 60 or 70 pounds (27 to 31.5 kilograms). *Coelophysis* had three clawed, grasping fingers on each hand. It also had slender jaws lined with sharp, curved, rough-edged teeth. Its name means "hollow form," for its thin-walled bones.

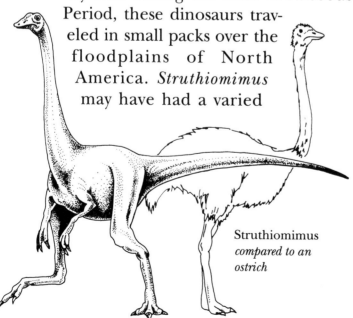

Coelophysis

STRUTHIOMIMUS *(strooth-ee-oh-MY-muss)*

"Ostrich mimic" is the meaning of this dinosaur's name, given because the animal slightly resembled a modern, flightless ostrich. It was a fast-paced, long-legged creature that was more than 11 feet (3.4 meters) long and stood about 7 feet (2.2 meters) tall. It is likely that during the Late Cretaceous Period, these dinosaurs traveled in small packs over the floodplains of North America. *Struthiomimus* may have had a varied

Struthiomimus
compared to an ostrich

diet that included plants, fruit, insects, small animals, and eggs, which it crunched with its toothless beak.

ORNITHOMIMUS *(or-nith-oh-MY-muss)*

Ornithomimus

The fossil remains of *Ornithomimus*, or "bird mimic," have been found in parts of North America. Most of this dinosaur's 11- to 12-foot (3.4- to 3.7-meter) length was made up by its long, flexible neck and its slender tail. *Ornithomimus* had sharp, curved claws at the tips of its three-fingered hands, and its snout ended in a toothless beak. The ornithomimosaur infraorder shares its name with this Late Cretaceous animal.

Ornithomimus's toothless beak

GALLIMIMUS *(gal-ih-MY-muss)*

This was the largest of the bird-mimic dinosaurs. It was about 13 to 20 feet (4 to 6.2 meters) long and may have weighed as much as 400 pounds (180 kilograms). Like its close relatives, *Gallimimus*, or "rooster mimic," had a small head that ended in a toothless snout. However, in one way it was different from other ornithomimosaurs. Its short arms and three-fingered hands weren't as well suited for grasping prey, so it might have relied mainly on leaves, fruit, and eggs for food.

Gallimimus

OVIRAPTOR (oh-vih-RAP-tor)

Oviraptor

The oviraptorosaur infraorder was named for this dinosaur. Its name means "egg stealer." A fossil of this Late Cretaceous animal was found in Asia over the nest of a *Protoceratops*. The scientists who found it thought that it might have somehow died while it was in the act of raiding the nest for eggs. *Oviraptor*'s deep skull and toothless beak were probably well suited for crushing eggs as well as for eating insects and berries. *Oviraptor* was a small dinosaur—only about 6 feet (1.9 meters) long—but it was swift and agile.

Oviraptor *skull fossil*

DINO FACT
Some dinosaurs, such as *Gallimimus*, may have been able to run in short bursts at speeds of up to 35 miles (56.4 kilometers) per hour.

FAST OR SLOW?

How do scientists figure out how fast dinosaurs could run? One way is by studying the length and shape of their bones. Speedy dinosaurs were usually lightly built for their size and had long hind legs and narrow feet. The bones in the faster dinosaurs' legs also show marks where powerful muscles were once attached.

Another way to figure out a dinosaur's speed is to measure its stride. For that, scientists need to find several preserved tracks. Stride is determined by measuring the distance between two prints made by the same foot. The faster the animal ran, the farther apart the prints will be. Of course, it is important to also know the length of the animal's hind leg, because a big, long-legged but slow dinosaur could have as lengthy a stride as a small, shorter-legged, speedy animal. (The length of the leg is approximately equal to four times the length of the foot.)

Fossilized dinosaur tracks help scientists tell how fast a dinosaur could run.

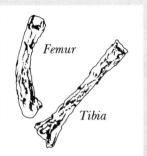

Coelophysis *bones*
(crushed specimens)

EDWIN HARRIS COLBERT

In 1942, this American paleontologist became the curator of reptiles of the Museum of Natural History in New York. He spent a great deal of time doing work in the field. His many accomplishments include the discovery of fifty new species of prehistoric animals, and the discovery of *Coelophysis* at Ghost Ranch, New Mexico. In 1969, Dr. Colbert and paleontologist Jim Jensen unearthed a mammal-like reptile, or therapsid, *Lystrosaurus*, in Antarctica, only 350 miles from the South Pole. Dr. Colbert is also the author of many popular books on dinosaurs, such as *Men and Dinosaurs* and *Dinosaurs: An Illustrated History*.

Procompsognathus

PROCOMPSOGNATHUS
(proh-komp-soh-NAY-thuss)

Procompsognathus is among the earliest-known dinosaurs and it is one of those that is difficult to classify. Its name means "before elegant jaw." That might seem a little odd, but the little dinosaur was given this title because it lived earlier than another of its relatives, *Compsognathus*. *Procompsognathus* lived during the Late Triassic Period. It stood about 1 foot (30.5 centimeters) high at the hips and was 4 feet (1.2 meters) long. It had a long, narrow snout and a long, flexible tail.

fossil skull of
Procompsognathus

Compsognathus

Compsognathus's
two-fingered hand

COMPSOGNATHUS *(komp-soh-NAY-thuss)*

Compsognathus means "elegant jaw." This animal was indeed gracefully built, from its little head to the tip of its slender tail. This tiny dinosaur is the only known member of its family group and one of the smallest adult dinosaurs ever found. *Compsognathus* was about 2 feet (61 centimeters) long and weighed about 5 pounds (2.3 kilograms). Still, it was probably an excellent hunter and could dart in and out of the undergrowth after its prey, gripping it with its small, clawed, two-fingered hands. During the Late Jurassic Period, *Compsognathus* roamed the shores of the warm, shallow seas that once covered what is now France and Germany.

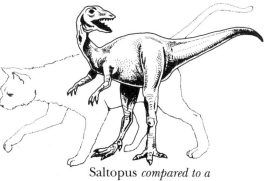

Saltopus *compared to a modern-day housecat*

SALTOPUS *(SALT-oh-puss)*

The adult *Salt-opus* was among the smallest of the Triassic dinosaurs. In fact, it was no bigger than a housecat. With its long tail included, this hard-to-classify little dinosaur measured only about 2 feet (61 centimeters) in length. It was a real lightweight, too, weighing in at about 3 or 4 pounds (1.4 to 1.8 kilograms). This tiny, Late Triassic predator was equipped with sharp teeth, which it probably used to grip such prey as small lizards and insects. *Saltopus,* or "leaping foot," was a speedy animal quite capable of running down a meal.

DINOSAUR NEIGHBORS: THE ICHTHYOSAURS

An ichthyosaur was a reptile that lived in the sea during the Mesozoic Era.

When dinosaurs ruled the land, reptiles also filled the seas. The ichthyosaurs (IK-thee-oh-sorz), or "fish lizards," were among the fastest creatures in the water. With powerful strokes of its strong tail, an ichthyosaur may have raced through the seas at speeds of 20 or 30 miles (32.2 or 48.3 kilometers) per hour. These ancient reptiles never left the water. In fact, they are one of the few fossil reptile groups that are confirmed to have given live birth. The young were born in the water and were probably nudged to the surface for their first breath of air.

WHY DO DOLPHINS AND ICHTHYOSAURS LOOK SO SIMILAR?

"Convergent evolution" is the term used to describe when unrelated animals develop similar traits to help them survive in their environment. For example, although they are not even distantly related, birds and bats have both developed wings to benefit from the advantages of flight.

Ancient ichthyosaurs lived in the ocean. Because they had to swim quickly to catch the fish they ate and to avoid being caught by their enemies, they developed a sleek, torpedo-shaped body, sturdy fins, and a powerful tail. Modern dolphins are mammals and are in no way related to ichthyosaurs, although they live in the ocean and eat fish, too. Dolphins also developed torpedo-shaped bodies, sturdy fins, and powerful tails. The similarity between dolphins and ichthyosaurs is an example of convergent evolution.

The ichthyosaur, an ancient reptile, and the dolphin, a modern mammal, have similar physical traits because of convergent evolution.

THE RISE OF PLANTS ON EARTH

Today, plants cover much of the land on Earth. But until about 410 million years ago, although plants and animals flourished in the sea, Earth's land was barren. The first pioneering plants to venture out of the safety of the sea were algae (AL-jee), which lived in tidal zones at the water's edge. It was a giant step, however, from the shoreline to land.

In the water, plants do not need strong stems because they float. They do not need roots, either, because they absorb nutrients from the water. Land plants need roots to gather water and nutrients from the soil. Land plants also need a system of tiny tubes in a sturdy stem to carry nutrients and water to all parts of the plant. Plants that follow this design are called vascular plants. The earliest known vascular plant was the 2-inch-tall (5.1-centimeter) *Cooksonia*.

When the age of the dinosaurs began about 227 million years ago, there were no flowering plants. The main types of plants were relatives of modern ferns, horsetails, palms, and pines. About 100 million years ago, during the Cretaceous Period, the first flowering plants appeared.

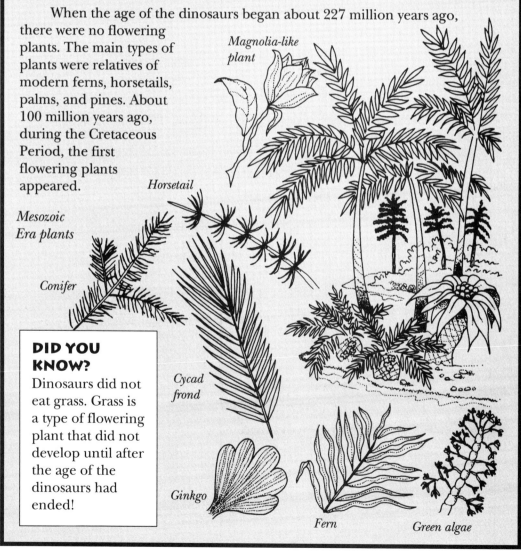

Magnolia-like plant

Horsetail

Mesozoic Era plants

Conifer

Cycad frond

Ginkgo

Fern

Green algae

DID YOU KNOW?

Dinosaurs did not eat grass. Grass is a type of flowering plant that did not develop until after the age of the dinosaurs had ended!

CHAPTER 2

DEADLY DINOSAURS

The Deinonychosaurs

Deinonychosaur (dy-NON-ih-kuh-sor) means "terrible-claw lizard." These medium-weight theropods had a curved claw on the second toe of each hind foot that was noticeably larger than the other claws. Like the ceratosaurs, these dinosaurs were speedy, agile, and lightly built for their size. They ran upright on their hind feet with their stiff tails outstretched for balance. The deinony-chosaurs had fairly short arms with grasping hands tipped with three-clawed fingers.

These predators were well equipped to capture and devour prey. They typically had short, deep skulls, powerful jaws, and sharp teeth—and they had something else in their favor, too. The deinonychosaurs generally had large brains, and may in fact have been the smartest and most cunning hunters of the Cretaceous Period. There is also some evidence that at least some of these fierce predators may have been warm-blooded.

DEINONYCHUS *(dy-NON-ih-kuss)*

clawed foot of Deinonychus

This creature, which was 10 to 13 feet (3.1 to 4 meters) long, may have been one of the most capable predators of the Cretaceous Period. It stood about 6 feet (1.9 meters) tall and weighed around 150 to 175 pounds (67.5 to 78.8 kilograms). It was fast and agile, and it probably hunted in small, deadly packs. From the size and

DISCOVERIES

Type of dinosaur and the modern name of the country in which it was found

DEINONYCHUS
• United States (in the Cloverly Formation, in Wyoming and Montana)

VELOCIRAPTOR
• Mongolia (in the Djadochta Formation, in Omnogov)
• China (in the Minhe Formation, in Inner Mongolia)

SAURORNITHOIDES
• Mongolia (in the Djadochta Formation and the Nemegt Forma-tion, in Omnogov)

DROMAEOSAURUS
• Canada (in the Judith River Formation, in Alberta)
• United States (in the Judith River Formation, in Montana)

TROÖDON
• Canada (in the Judith River Formation and the Horseshoe Canyon Formation, in Alberta)
• United States (in the Judith River Formation and the Hell Creek For-mation, in Montana, and in the Lance For-mation, in Wyoming)

Deinonychus

MAJOR FINDS

In 1964, Dr. John Ostrom and his assistant, Grant E. Meyer, were searching for fossils in the hill country of Montana. They found something that would forever change the way people viewed dinosaurs. Poking out of the hard ground was the large, curved claw of an unknown type of dinosaur. As more of the creature was uncovered, including several of its sharp, jagged-edged teeth, it became clear that this animal didn't fit the image of a slow, sluggish dinosaur. Instead, it had been an agile, active hunter that had used its lethal claw as a weapon to tear at its victims. The dinosaur that was discovered on that day some 30 years ago was introduced to the world as *Deinonychus*, or "terrible claw."

John Ostrom

shape of its skull, scientists have determined that *Deinonychus* was probably quite intelligent and had excellent vision. These traits are a big advantage for a hunter. This dinosaur had an arsenal of sharp, curved teeth and claws, but the large, curved claw on the second toe of each foot was its most lethal weapon. During an attack, *Deinonychus*, or "terrible claw," used its pair of 5-inch-long (12.7-centimeter) talons to slash and rip apart its victim.

VELOCIRAPTOR (vuh-LOSS-ih-rap-tor)

Velociraptor *head*

The name of this dinosaur means "speedy thief." *Velociraptor* moved rapidly over the desert in what is now Asia during the Late Cretaceous Period. Unlike many of its close relatives, it had a long, low head and a flattened snout. It was generally about 6 feet (1.9 meters) long. It is believed that *Velociraptor* had an appetite for eggs, snatching them from the nests of other dinosaurs. The remains of a *Velociraptor* were found with those of a *Protoceratops*.

The two were locked in a death struggle. Perhaps the battle began when the *Protoceratops* discovered the predator robbing its nest.

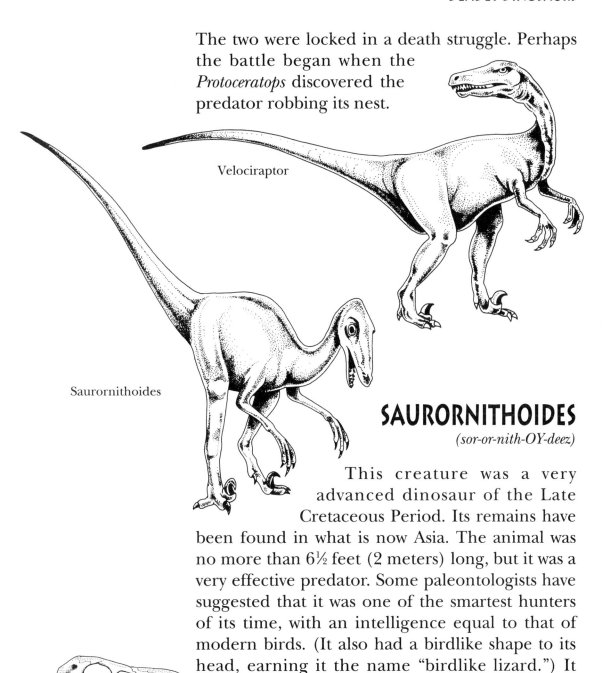

Velociraptor

Saurornithoides

Saurornithoides
skull fossil

SAURORNITHOIDES
(sor-or-nith-OY-deez)

This creature was a very advanced dinosaur of the Late Cretaceous Period. Its remains have been found in what is now Asia. The animal was no more than 6½ feet (2 meters) long, but it was a very effective predator. Some paleontologists have suggested that it was one of the smartest hunters of its time, with an intelligence equal to that of modern birds. (It also had a birdlike shape to its head, earning it the name "birdlike lizard.") It may have had another advantage over other larger predators. *Saurornithoides* had large eyes and may have had binocular vision, much like that of today's wolves and hawks, which would have allowed it to judge distance more accurately. It is even possible that this dinosaur hunted in the dim light of dusk.

DROMAEOSAURUS (drom-ee-oh-SOR-uss)

sickle-shaped claw on
Dromaeosaurus's foot

This Late Cretaceous dinosaur was about 6 feet (1.9 meters) long and weighed about 100 pounds (45 kilograms). Uncovered in Canada in 1914, it was the first dinosaur of the midsized theropods to be discovered. Like others in this group, it had a large, sickle-shaped claw on each foot. After ambushing or perhaps chasing down its prey, *Dromaeosaurus* probably balanced nimbly on one foot as it slashed at its victim's flesh with the other. Its name means "running lizard," and with its long legs and lightweight body, this animal may have reached running speeds of 25 miles (40.3 kilometers) an hour or more.

Dromaeosaurus

TROÖDON (TROH-oh-don)

narrow claws on
Troödon's hand

The name *Troödon* means "wound tooth." Its serrated teeth were certainly sharp and quite capable of ripping and tearing flesh. This small, Late Cretaceous dinosaur was about 6 feet (1.9 meters) long and may have weighed as little as 30 to 60 pounds (13.5 to 27 kilograms). The areas of its brain devoted to the senses and reflexes, however, were comparatively large and well developed, so it was likely to have been a formidable hunter.

Troödon was one of the first North American dinosaurs named, and scientists now believe that this agile dinosaur and a creature once known as *Stenonychosaurus* are actually the same animal.

Troödon

DINO FACT

There is evidence, such as fossilized tracks, suggesting that many small and medium-sized meat-eaters hunted in packs. Hunting in a pack is a good strategy, because several predators working together can capture and kill even very large prey. One of the animals preyed upon by *Deinonychus*, for example, was *Tenontosaurus*, a 20-foot-long (6.2-meter) plant-eater that weighed up to 4,000 pounds (1,800 kilograms).

A pack of Deinonychus *work together to bring down their prey, a* Tenontosaurus.

33

BIRDS: THE MODERN DINOSAURS

Dr. John Ostrom once commented that the dinosaurs did not die off but simply flew away. What he meant was that the dinosaurs may still be represented on Earth by their direct ancestors—the birds. Many paleontologists now believe that birds are related in some way to the dinosaurs, and that our modern feathered friends may have developed from small theropods. Recently, the remains of an unusual creature called *Mononychus* (muh-NON-ih-kuss) were discovered in the Gobi Desert in Asia. This animal looked like a small, turkey-sized theropod, but it had many traits of both dinosaurs and birds. It had a long tail, but its breastbone and wrist bones were similar to those of birds. It may even have had feathers!

The Mononychus *exhibited traits of both dinosaurs and modern birds.*

WERE THE DINOSAURS WARM-BLOODED OR COLD-BLOODED?

Modern birds and mammals have a built-in system for keeping their bodies warm, no matter what the temperature around them might be. By "burning" the food they eat, these warm-blooded animals produce body heat. Other creatures, such as fish, amphibians, and reptiles, are cold-blooded and do not have a built-in system for controlling body temperature. They warm up or cool down depending on the temperature of their outside environment. For instance, when a lizard wants to warm up, it may crawl up on a rock and bask in the sun. If it wants to cool off, it might hide in the shade beneath the rock.

Because dinosaurs are thought to have been reptiles, scientists initially guessed that they must all have been cold-blooded. Now, many scientists are changing their minds. Some dinosaurs, though not truly warm-blooded, might have had special ways of conserving body heat. Other dinosaurs, such as the very active small and medium-sized theropods, might actually have been warm-blooded. The important thing to remember in this debate is that there were many different varieties of dinosaurs, and, like modern mammals, they surely had different ways of staying warm or cool.

CHAPTER 3

LORDS OF THE MESOZOIC

The Carnosaurs

Quick—think of a huge, flesh-eating dinosaur. Did you picture *Tyrannosaurus rex*? Most people do. This ferocious beast belonged to a whole group of large theropods called the carnosaurs, which means "meat-eating lizards." Generally these were large, bulky animals that walked upright on strong hind legs. Carnosaurs had short, muscular arms, each typically ending in two or three fingers (though some families had more) tipped with curved, razor-sharp claws. The typical carnosaur also had a very large head, a fairly short neck, and jaws lined with long, ragged-edged teeth that were perfect for slicing through flesh.

TYRANNOSAURUS *(ty-ran-oh-SOR-uss)*

Tyrannosaurus
skull fossil

Tyrannosaurus was among the largest of the carnosaurs. When it stood on its hind legs, it reached nearly 20 feet (6.2 meters) in height. Its average length from nose to tail was probably about 40 feet (12.4 meters). Scientists estimate that a full-grown *Tyrannosaurus* weighed between 8,000 and 16,000 pounds (3,600 and 7,200 kilograms).

Tyrannosaurus, or "tyrant lizard," had roughly sixty teeth reaching 3 to 7 inches (7.6 to 17.8 centimeters) in length, which it used to tear apart meat. Although some paleontologists suggest that this huge Cretaceous creature may have been a scavenger that fed on the

Tyrannosaurus

remains of dead animals, most feel it was a capable and deadly predator. The remains of the most well-known species, *Tyrannosaurus rex*, are found in the western United States. One other species is known from discoveries in Asia.

DINOSAUR MYSTERY

Tyrannosaurus rex may have been the largest land predator ever to have walked the earth, at about 40 feet (12.4 meters) from nose to tail. Strangely, however, its arms were only about 3 feet (.93 meter) in length—no longer than those of an adult human. Because this creature's short arms couldn't even reach its mouth, it seems unlikely that it used them for grasping and holding prey. One suggestion is that the small but muscular arms were used to help the animal rise to its feet after a snooze. What do you think?

Tyrannosaurus's arms were no longer than those of an adult human.

ALBERTOSAURUS *(al-BER-toh-sor-uss)*

Albertosaurus's foot

Albertosaurus (also known as *Gorgosaurus*) was named for the province of Alberta, Canada, where the remains of this Late Cretaceous dinosaur were first discovered. About 11 feet (3.4 meters) tall, 26 feet (8.1 meters) long, and 6,000 pounds (2,700 kilograms) in weight, it was smaller than its close cousins, but it was probably no less fierce.

In fact, *Albertosaurus* may have been a little faster and more agile than other, larger carnosaurs.

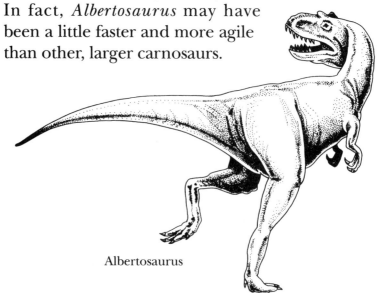

Albertosaurus

MEGALOSAURUS *(meg-uh-loh-SOR-uss)*

jaw bone fossil of Megalosaurus

The name *Megalosaurus* means "big lizard." This Jurassic dinosaur roamed the seaside forests of what is now England and France. It was about 10 feet (3.1 meters) tall and 30 feet (9.3 meters) long, and it weighed from 2,000 to 4,000 pounds (900 to 1,800 kilograms). The creature had a

---

DISCOVERIES

Type of dinosaur and the modern name of the country in which it was found

TYRANNOSAURUS
• Canada (in the Scollard Formation and Willow Creek Formation, in Alberta, and in the Frenchman Formation, in Saskatchewan)
• United States (in the Hell Creek Formation, in Montana and South Dakota; in the Livingston Formation, in Montana; in the Lance Formation, in Wyoming; in the Laramie and Denver Formations, in Colorado; in the Javelina Formation, in Texas; and in the McRae Formation, in New Mexico)
• China (in the Qiuba Formation, in the province of Henan, and in the Subashi Formation, in the province of Xinjiang Uygur Zizhiqu)
• Mongolia (in the Nemegt Formation, in Omnogov, and in the White Beds of Kareem, in Bayankhongor)

ALBERTOSAURUS
• Canada (in the Judith River Formation, in Alberta)
• United States (in the Judith River Formation, in Montana, and in the Fruitland Formation, in New Mexico)

MEGALOSAURUS
• England (in the Chipping Norton Formation, the Stonesfield Slate, and the Cornbrash Formation, in Oxfordshire; in the Chipping Norton Formation, in Gloucestershire; in the Great Oolite, in Wiltshire; and in the Corallian Oolite Formation, in North Yorkshire)
• France (in the Department of Indre)

ALLOSAURUS
• United States (in the Morrison Formation, in Colorado, Utah, Montana, Wyoming, South Dakota, Oklahoma, and New Mexico)

SPINOSAURUS
• Egypt (in the Baharija Formation, near Marsa Matruh, in the Qattara Depression)

large head with powerful jaws, and its sharp, curved, saw-edged teeth were excellent weapons. *Megalosaurus* has a special claim to fame. In 1824, it was the first dinosaur publicly described and named as a representative of the meat-eating group of dinosaurs.

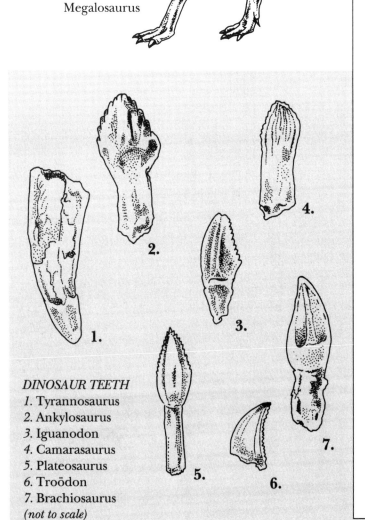

Megalosaurus

DINOSAUR TEETH
1. Tyrannosaurus
2. Ankylosaurus
3. Iguanodon
4. Camarasaurus
5. Plateosaurus
6. Troödon
7. Brachiosaurus
(not to scale)

TEETH

Meat-eating dinosaurs had something important in common. Almost all of them had strong jaws with an arsenal of sharp teeth. These teeth grew continuously, and when they were worn out or lost, they were replaced by new teeth.

The shape and arrangement of a dinosaur's teeth give scientists many important clues about how the animal lived. For example, sharp, pointed teeth usually belonged to meat-eaters, while plant-eaters often had weak, stubby teeth or flattened grinding teeth. To the left are the teeth of several different types of dinosaurs. What can you guess about these creatures just by studying their teeth?

HOW DO SCIENTISTS FIGURE OUT HOW MUCH A DINOSAUR WEIGHED?

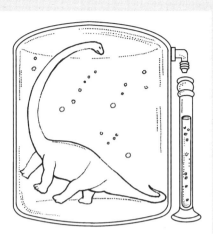

A model of a dinosaur is submerged in water to determine how much the animal weighed.

One way is to make a scale model of the dinosaur based on what is known about it. The researcher then dunks the model in a container of water to see how much water is displaced. Since animals are generally about the same density as water, they displace their own weight. By measuring how much water is displaced by the model, the scientist can figure out the dinosaur's weight.

ALLOSAURUS (al-oh-SOR-uss)

Allosaurus's *neck vertebra*

The unusual shape of the bones in its spine gave *Allosaurus,* or "different lizard," its name. This Jurassic predator was equipped with a mouthful of 2- to 4-inch-long (5.1- to 10.2-centimeter) teeth, designed for ripping flesh. It was about 35 feet (10.9 meters) long and weighed from 4,000 to 8,000 pounds (1,800 to 3,600 kilograms). This creature has been fairly well studied. In one area of Utah alone, the partial remains of some sixty of these dinosaurs were uncovered.

Allosaurus

SPINOSAURUS *(spy-noh-SOR-uss)*

Spinosaurus *bones*

tibia

During the Cretaceous Period, the land that is now part of North Africa was home to this large carnosaur. It was as much as 40 feet (12.4 meters) long and may have weighed up to 14,000 pounds (6,300 kilograms). Like other carnosaurs it had sharp teeth and strong, curved claws, but it had something else that no other meat-eater known had. On its back, *Spinosaurus* sported a long, tall sail, or fin, of leathery skin supported by stiff spines. In fact, that is how this dinosaur got its name. The sail is believed to have helped this dinosaur to control its body temperature. For instance, when it wanted to warm up, it might have turned the sail to face the sun.

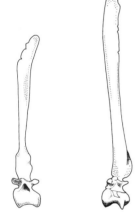

dorsal vertebrae

Spinosaurus

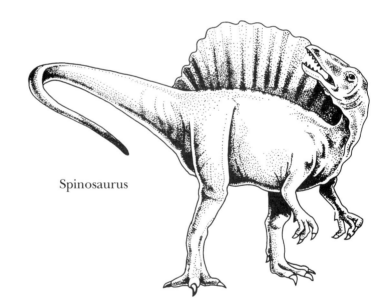

MAKING A *TYRANNOSAURUS* MASK

Here's a quick and easy way to make a *Tyranno-saurus* snout with only a paper cup, scissors, a pencil or marker, and some string.

1. Draw a line of sharp, daggerlike teeth at the base of the cup.

2. Use scissors to punch a whole in the bottom of the cup and carefully cut out around the toothy outline.

1.

3. Punch two small holes, one on either side of the cup, and tie a 12-inch-long (30.5-centimeter) piece of twine through each.

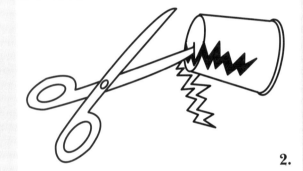

2.

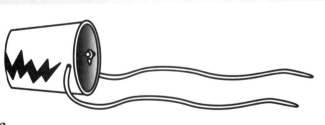

Now place the toothy mask over your own nose and mouth, and tie the two loose ends of string behind your head.

3.

CHAPTER 4

EARLY DINOSAURS
The Prosauropods

The first members of the infraorder of Prosauropoda (which means "before sauropods") showed up early in the dinosaur age. Some of these creatures were small, but others may have been as long as 30 feet (9 meters) from nose to tail. No matter what their size, however, the prosauropods had some characteristics in common. They had long, flexible necks, long tails, and small heads.

These primitive dinosaurs of the Late Triassic and Early Jurassic periods belonged to the suborder Sauropodomorpha. The earliest prosauropods were among the smallest dinosaurs and were usually lightly built. Some may have eaten both meat and plants. They also may have been comfortable walking on either two legs or four. The later prosauropods were larger, and the biggest of these most certainly walked with all four feet firmly on the ground. It's also likely that these later prosauropods ate only plants.

ANCHISAURUS *(AN-kee-sor-uss)*

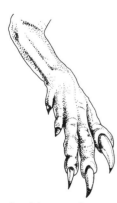

Anchisaurus's five-fingered hand

"Near lizard" is what this dinosaur's name means. During the Late Triassic to Early Jurassic periods, when *Anchisaurus* roamed the Earth, the land was joined into one huge continent. This slim-bodied dinosaur was about 8 feet (2.5 meters) in length and weighed around 60 pounds (27 kilograms).

DISCOVERIES

Type of dinosaur and the modern name of the country in which it was found

ANCHISAURUS
• United States (in the Upper Beds, Newark Supergroup, in Connecticut and Massachusetts)

MUSSAURUS
• Argentina (in the El Tranquillo Formation, in the province of Santa Cruz)

RIOJASAURUS
• Argentina (in the Upper Los Colorados Formation, in the province of La Rioja, and in the Quebrada del Baro Formation, in the province of San Juan)

PLATEOSAURUS
• Germany (in Knollenmergel, in the state of Baden-Württemberg, and in Niedersachsen, Feuerletten, in the state of Bavaria)
• Switzerland (Obere Bunte Mergel, in the canton of Aargau)
• France (in the Marnes irisées supérieurs, in the Department of Jura and in the Department of Doubs)

EFRASSIA
• Germany (in Unterer and Mittlerer Stübensandstein, in the state of Baden-Württemberg)

MASSOSPONDYLUS
• South Africa (in the Upper Elliot Formation and Clarens Formation, in the Orange Free State Province and Cape Province, and in the Bushveld Sandstone in the Transvaal Province)
• Lesotho (in the Upper Elliot Formation)
• Zimbabwe (in the Forest Sandstone)

It was probably a plant-eater that munched on ferns and horsetails, perhaps using the large claw on the first finger of each five-fingered hand to root up plants.

Anchisaurus

MUSSAURUS *(moo-SOR-uss)*

One of the smallest dinosaurs ever found was a newly hatched *Mussaurus,* or "mouse lizard." This baby dinosaur was no more than 8 inches (20.3 centimeters) long. The hatchling was discovered in the remains of a ground nest that held other hatchlings and two little eggs, each only 1 inch (2.5 centimeters) long. If it had lived to be an adult, *Mussaurus* could have reached 10 feet (3.1 meters) in length.

Mussaurus *in nest*

RIOJASAURUS *(ree-OH-huh-sor-uss)*

hind foot of
Riojasaurus

Discovered in the La Rioja Province of Argentina, *Riojasaurus* was between 20 and 35 feet (6.2 to 10.9 meters) long. A sturdy, large-bodied animal with heavy legs, it walked solidly on all four feet to support its weight. Because of its very long neck, it had an advantage over other prosauropods. *Riojasaurus* was probably able to munch the tops of some plants that were far out of the reach of its smaller relatives.

Riojasaurus

PLATEOSAURUS *(play-tee-oh-SOR-uss)*

fossil Plateosaurus
skull

The remains of *Plateosaurus*, or "flat lizard," have been found in rocks formed from the sands of the Late Triassic deserts. It was a fairly large animal that reached lengths of 20 feet (6.2 meters) or more. Although it was stocky and heavily built, it was probably able to rear up on its hind legs when it wanted to. It may have done this to browse on the leaves of plants, slicing them off with its small, leaf-shaped teeth.

Plateosaurus

EFRASSIA *(eh-FRAH-see-uh)*

Efrassia's hand

Efrassia was a typical early prosauropod, with a long neck and tail and a small head. This plant-eater had grasping hands for gripping leaves when it reared up on its hind feet to browse. It was also quite capable of walking or running on all four legs when it needed to. *Efrassia* was named for E. Frass, a German fossil collector who found the first remains of this dinosaur in 1909.

Efrassia

MASSOSPONDYLUS *(mass-oh-SPOND-ih-luss)*

five-fingered hand of Massospondylus

This Late Triassic dinosaur's name means "bulky vertebrae," but it was actually lightly built. It was about 13 feet (4 meters) long and had a very long, flexible neck. *Massospondylus*'s teeth were suited for eating both meat and plants. It may have used its five-fingered hands to grip branches and to grasp small prey. Its hands were also suitable for walking, and it probably strolled along easily on either two legs or four.

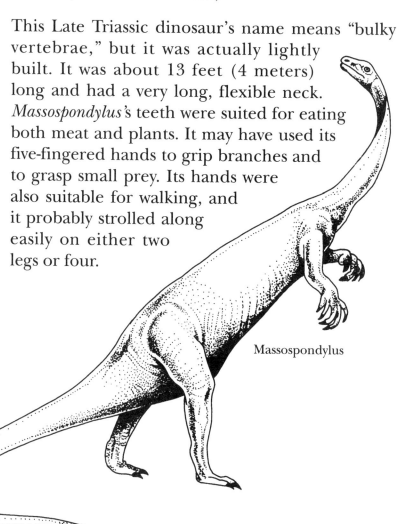

Massospondylus

DINOSAUR NEIGHBORS: THE EARLIEST MAMMALS

Mammals can be found throughout the oceans and on every continent on Earth. Today, the mammal group includes some of the largest and most powerful creatures on the planet. During the dinosaur age, however, mammals were small, rodentlike creatures that probably hid in the shadows or in trees, coming out only after dark to search for a meal of insects.

One example of an early mammal is *Megazostrodon* (meg-uh-ZAHS-troh-don). This little creature lived during the Late Triassic and Early Jurassic periods. It is identified as a mammal because it had four different kinds of teeth, which grew in two sets, and it seems to have had a covering of fur. The distant relatives of *Megazostrodon* can still be found on Earth today as the monotremes, which include Australia's duck-billed platypus and echidna. Although they are mammals, these animals lay eggs. It's likely that *Megazostrodon* laid eggs as well, but, like all mammals do, they probably nourished their offspring with milk from the mother's body once the eggs had hatched.

DINO FACT
Eighty percent of all mammals living today are smaller than the smallest dinosaur.

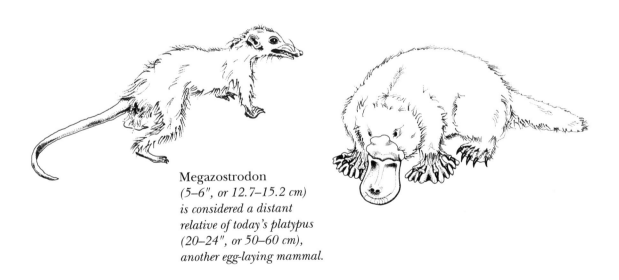

Megazostrodon
(5–6", or 12.7–15.2 cm)
is considered a distant
relative of today's platypus
(20–24", or 50–60 cm),
another egg-laying mammal.

WHICH WAS THE FIRST DINOSAUR?

This isn't an easy question to answer, because the fossil record we have of life at the beginning of the Mesozoic Era is incomplete. Still, there are two dinosaurs that are certainly among the oldest known.

Herrerasaurus (her-ray-rah-SOR-uss) lived in the Mid-Triassic Period, about 230 million years ago, in what is now Argentina. This fairly small animal was between 6 to 8 feet (1.9 to 2.5 meters) in length and weighed about 300 pounds (135 kilograms). *Herrerasaurus* was probably an agile predator that ran swiftly on two legs. Some paleontologists believe that it will prove to be the oldest known saurischian. It was named in honor of a member of the team that first discovered its remains.

Staurikosaurus (stor-IK-oh-sor-uss) means "cross lizard." It was named for the Southern Cross, a constellation that can be seen only from the Southern Hemisphere. The remains of this dinosaur were discovered in Brazil. It was a bipedal (two-legged) meat-eater. Although it was probably a fierce predator, *Staurikosaurus* was only about 6 feet (1.9 meters) long and weighed about 65 pounds (29.3 kilograms).

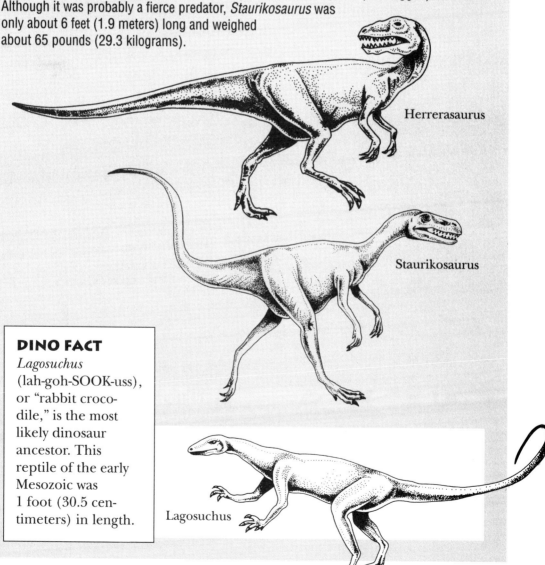

Herrerasaurus

Staurikosaurus

Lagosuchus

DINO FACT
Lagosuchus (lah-goh-SOOK-uss), or "rabbit crocodile," is the most likely dinosaur ancestor. This reptile of the early Mesozoic was 1 foot (30.5 centimeters) in length.

CHAPTER 5

GENTLE GIANTS
The Sauropods

The plant-eating giants of the dinosaur age were members of the suborder Sauropodomorpha and the infraorder Sauropoda, or "lizard-footed" dinosaurs. The smallest of the adults was no less than 30 feet (9.3 meters) in length, while the largest was probably nearly half a city block long. These creatures thundered across lowlands and floodplains mainly during the Jurassic Period. After that time many—but not all—of the sauropods died out.

The sauropods had long, slender necks and tails, and small heads with weak, blunt teeth. They were bulky creatures with powerful, pillarlike legs and wide, flat feet. Because of their tremendous size and weight, these dinosaurs were limited to walking on four feet. However, some may have been able to rear up onto their hind feet to browse for leaves or perhaps to fend off an attacker.

APATOSAURUS *(uh-PAT-oh-sor-uss)*

Apatosaurus was given its name, which means "deceptive lizard," because its backbones, or vertebrae, closely resembled those of another reptile. This Jurassic dinosaur is one of the best-known plant-eaters of the dinosaur age. One reason for its popularity is its size. From nose to tail, *Apatosaurus* measured as much as 70 feet (21.7 meters) long. It was at least 15 feet (4.7 meters) high at the hips, and it weighed more than 60,000 pounds (27,000 kilograms)!

DISCOVERIES

Type of dinosaur and the modern name of the country in which it was found

APATOSAURUS
• United States (in the Morrison Formation, in Colorado, Wyoming, Utah, and Oklahoma)

CAMARASAURUS
• United States (in the Morrison Formation, in Wyoming, Colorado, New Mexico, Montana, and Utah)

BRACHIOSAURUS
• United States (in the Morrison Formation, in Colorado and Utah)
• Tanzania (in the Tendaguru Beds, in the Mtwara region)

ALAMOSAURUS
• United States (in the Upper Kirtland Shale, in New Mexico; the North Horn Formation, in Utah; and the Javelina Formation and El Picacho Formation, in Texas)

DIPLODOCUS
• United States (in the Morrison Formation, in Colorado, Utah, and Wyoming)

SALTASAURUS
• Argentina (in the Lecho Formation, in the province of Salta, and in the Colorado Formation, in the province of Rio Negro)

MAMENCHISAURUS
• China (in the Shangshaximiao Formation, in Sichuan Province)

Of course, it took a lot of plants to fill up such a huge creature. *Apatosaurus* spent most of its time browsing to find as much as 500 pounds (225 kilograms) of food every day. With its long neck, this dinosaur was able to reach high into the treetops, where it used its small, peglike teeth to rake the leaves from branches.

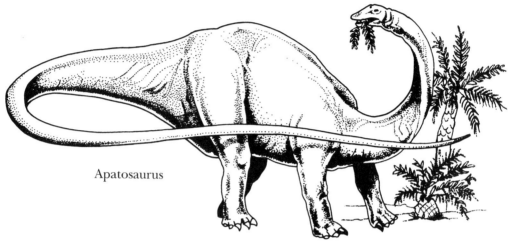

Apatosaurus

CAMARASAURUS *(KAM-ah-ruh-sor-uss)*

Compared to other sauropods, *Camarasaurus* was small. Adults grew to between 30 and 60 feet (9.3 to 18.6 meters) in length, and their tails and necks were much shorter than those of their relatives. But *Camarasaurus* excelled in other ways. The jaws of its short, boxy skull were lined with strong teeth that were excellent for chomping tough plant matter. Its short tail also seems to have been quite powerful and may have been

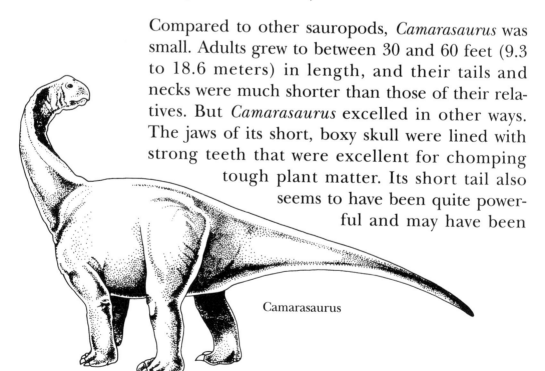

Camarasaurus

fossil skull of
Camarasaurus

an effective defense against predators. During the Jurassic Period, *Camarasaurus* probably roamed across the floodplains in impressive herds, with the youngsters traveling along safely under the protection of the adults.

THE CONFUSION OVER *APATOSAURUS*

You may have heard this animal called by another name—*Brontosaurus*. That means "thunder lizard." It was called that because early paleontologists mistakenly thought its huge size meant that the ground rumbled under the feet of this giant as it walked. *Brontosaurus* was the name given to the remains of a dinosaur discovered by O. C. Marsh. It turns out, however, that the remains matched those of an animal Marsh had already described and named *Apatosaurus*. Once the mistake was discovered, scientists agreed to use the original name.

That wasn't the only confusion over this giant dinosaur. It seems that when Marsh tried to put the remains of *Apatosaurus* together, he reconstructed it with the wrong head! He used the skull of another sauropod, *Camarasaurus*, that had been found far away in another state. The mistake wasn't corrected until nearly 100 years later, in 1979, when several paleontologists took a closer look at the fossil evidence.

Apatosaurus *with* Camarasaurus *head*

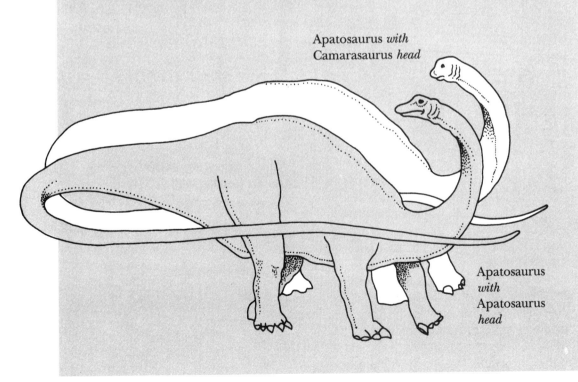

Apatosaurus *with* Apatosaurus *head*

BRACHIOSAURUS *(BRAK-ee-oh-sor-uss)*

Brachiosaurus's head, with nostrils over eyes

This huge beast may have been up to 85 feet (26.4 meters) long and 40 feet (12.4 meters) tall—nearly the height of a four-story building! *Brachiosaurus* weighed in at as much as 160,000 pounds (72,000 kilograms). Its name, which means "arm lizard," comes from the fact that the forelegs (or arms) of this dinosaur were much longer than its hind legs. The position of its nostrils—centered above its eyes—originally led some scientists to believe that the creature spent most of its time in water, with only its head above the surface. Now we know, however, that it was a land dweller.

Brachiosaurus

O. C. Marsh

O. C. MARSH AND EDWARD COPE: THE BONE WARS

Before Othniel Charles Marsh and Edward Drinker Cope appeared on the scene, only nine types of North American dinosaurs were known. The rivalry between these two nineteenth-century scientists, however, helped to raise that number to more than one hundred. Their rivalry was known as the Bone Wars. Marsh and Cope began as friends, both searching the North American West for the remains of dinosaurs. But the search quickly became a competition. Each man hired teams of fossil hunters and diggers to comb rocky outcrops for new and exciting finds. The scientists ended up as bitter rivals, but their contribution to paleontology was remarkable. Among the dinosaurs first described by O. C. Marsh are *Diplodocus*, *Stegosaurus*, and *Triceratops*. Among the dinosaurs described by Edward Cope are *Camarasaurus*, *Monoclonius*, and *Coelophysis*.

Edward Cope

ALAMOSAURUS *(al-uh-moh-SOR-uss)*

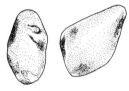

stomach stones (gastroliths)

This "Alamo lizard" is among the sauropods that lived at the end of the Cretaceous Period. Although it was fairly small for a sauropod, measuring between 50 and 70 feet (15.5 to 21.7 meters) in length, it was still a giant when compared to many other Cretaceous dinosaurs. Like other sauropods, this dinosaur probably just nipped off the plants and leaves it ate and swallowed them without chewing. It's likely that *Alamosaurus* also swallowed rough stones, which would roll around its stomach, mashing the leaves and aiding in digestion. Scientists call these stomach stones gastroliths.

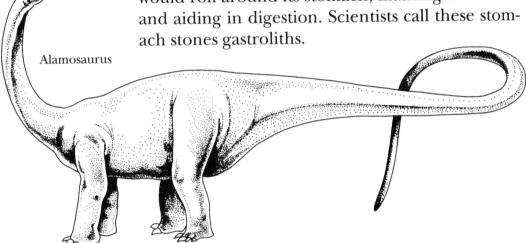

Alamosaurus

DIPLODOCUS *(dih-PLOD-oh-kuss)*

Diplodocus skull fossil

Although *Diplodocus* measured an amazing 85 to 100 feet (26.4 to 31 meters) in length, it was very lightly built, weighing only about 20,000 to 24,000 pounds (9,000 to 10,800 kilograms). Much of this dinosaur's length was in its 30-foot-long (9.3-meter) neck, and 45-foot-long (14-meter), whip-like tail. Size alone was probably the best defense for *Diplodocus*, but it may also have warded off attackers with its tail, which could be moved back and forth. The creature had broad, flat feet, and the inner toe of each front foot was equipped with a thick, curved claw. The name *Diplodocus* means "double beam" and refers to the structure of certain bones in the animal's tail.

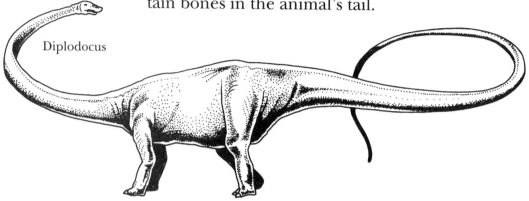

Diplodocus

SALTASAURUS *(sahl-tuh-SOR-uss)*

horned spike on Saltasaurus*'s back*

Named for the area where its remains were discovered, the "Salta lizard" lived in what is now Argentina. This dinosaur is quite special for several reasons. For one thing, it lived during the Cretaceous Period, when many of the other sauropods had already disappeared. It measured up to 39 feet (12.1 meters) in length, and it weighed between 12,000 and 20,000 pounds (5,400 to 9,000 kilograms). This creature is the first sauropod known to have armor: The skin of its back and flanks was covered with bony plates, studs, and tiny horned spikes.

Saltasaurus

MAMENCHISAURUS *(muh-MUN-chee-sor-uss)*

This dinosaur's claim to fame is that it had the longest neck of any known animal. Its neck was 36 feet (11.2 meters) long! Because of the animal's bone structure, however, its neck was not very flexible. *Mamenchisaurus* was about 60 to 70 feet (18.6 to 21.7 meters) long and it weighed 60,000 pounds (27,000 kilograms). If it could have risen up on its hind legs, as many Jurassic sauropods could, it would have been able to reach leaves that were growing five stories above the ground! *Mamenchisaurus* was named for the province in China where it was first discovered in 1952.

Mamenchisaurus

full skeleton of
Mamenchisaurus

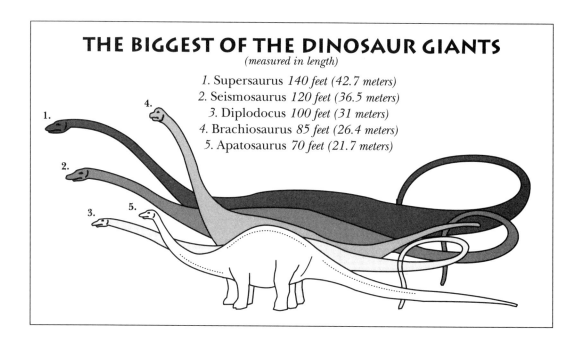

THE BIGGEST OF THE DINOSAUR GIANTS
(measured in length)

1. Supersaurus *140 feet (42.7 meters)*
2. Seismosaurus *120 feet (36.5 meters)*
3. Diplodocus *100 feet (31 meters)*
4. Brachiosaurus *85 feet (26.4 meters)*
5. Apatosaurus *70 feet (21.7 meters)*

DINOSAUR NEIGHBORS: THE PTEROSAURS

One thing that no dinosaur ever had was wings. Still, the Mesozoic skies were not empty. Insects certainly buzzed through the air, and winged reptiles called pterosaurs (TAYR-uh-sorz) probably swooped after them. Pterosaurs were not ancient birds or bats, but a unique type of lightly built creature that flew on leathery wings of skin.

Over the entire Mesozoic Era there were about 80 different kinds of pterosaurs. Those that took to the skies early in the era were called the rhamphorhynchoids (ram-foh-RINK-oydz). They were generally no bigger than large hawks. A rhamphorhynchoid usually had a short neck and a long, slender tail. The tail often had a blade of bone at the end that may have served as a rudder.

Rhamphorhynchus

The pterodactyloids (tayr-uh-DAK-til-oydz) showed up late in the Jurassic Period. These creatures had long necks and very short tails. Some were small, but others grew to tremendous sizes. *Quetzal-coatlus* (ket-zal-koh-AHT-luss) lived during the Late Cretaceous Period. It had a 10-foot-long (3.1-meter) neck, and a wingspan of nearly 40 feet (12.4 meters).

Pterodactylus

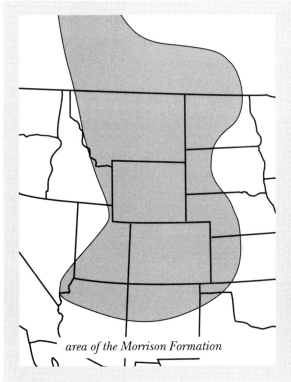

area of the Morrison Formation

WHERE ON EARTH?

The Morrison Formation is a band of Late Jurassic rocks that stretches along the Rocky Mountains from Montana to New Mexico. The first dinosaur remains discovered in the formation were found in 1877 near Morrison, Colorado. Since then, almost all of the Late Jurassic dinosaur remains uncovered in North America have come from this formation.

During the time of the dinosaurs, this area was covered by dry floodplains. It bordered a narrow inland waterway, called the Sundance Sea, that stretched from the Arctic Ocean to what is now southern Utah. The area had distinct dry and rainy seasons, and charcoal deposits hint of ancient forest fires that were probably caused by lightning.

PART III: THE ORNITHISCHIANS

The ornithischians are known as the bird-hipped dinosaurs because the arrangement of their hipbones is similar to that of modern birds. The pubis and ischium bones in the hips of these dinosaurs both pointed backward. *Triceratops* and *Stegosaurus* belonged to this dinosaur group.

These bird-hipped dinosaurs were plant-eaters. They came in a wide variety of shapes and sizes and are divided into at least four suborders.

THE BIRD-HIPPED DINOSAUR FAMILY TREE

Order	Ornithischia
Suborder	Stegosauria Ornithopoda Pachycephalosauria Ankylosauria Ceratopsia

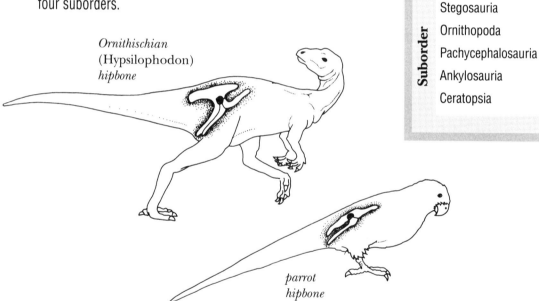

Ornithischian (Hypsilophodon) hipbone

parrot hipbone

Suborder	Description	Example
Stegosauria	plates and/or spikes; four-legged	*Stegosaurus*
Ornithopoda	larger members four-legged, but stood or ran on two legs; smaller members two-legged	*Iguanodon*
Pachycephalosauria	two-legged; skull thick at crown	*Pachycephalosaurus*
Ankylosauria	armored; four-legged	*Ankylosaurus*
Ceratopsia	horns and bony neck frills; four-legged	*Triceratops*

CHAPTER 6

PLATES AND SPIKES
The Stegosaurs

The stegosaurs, members of the bird-hipped ornithischian order, were different from other dinosaurs in that each variety of stegosaur had a single or double row of bony plates or spines along its back. The number, shape, and arrangement of the plates were different for each type of stegosaur. These dinosaurs' powerful tails were also equipped with long, sharp spikes, which the animals used to defend themselves against predators.

The fairly large, plant-eating stegosaurs were sturdy, slow-moving animals. They probably browsed on low-growing branches for food. Most had small, narrow heads, with jaws that ended in tough, toothless beaks. Small, weak, leaf-shaped teeth lined the sides of their jaws.

The stegosaurs lasted more than 50 million years and were most widespread during the Middle to Late Jurassic Period, though some lived into the Cretaceous Period. Many scientists believe that the stegosaurs died out because of the rapid rise of the ankylosaur, a type of dinosaur that was successful at competing with the stegosaurs for food.

HUAYANGOSAURUS
(hwah-YANG-oh-sor-uss)

Huayangosaurus's shoulder spike

Huayangosaurus is one of the oldest known stegosaurs. It lived sometime during the Mid-Jurassic Period. Unlike other stegosaurs, this animal appears to have had some teeth in the front of its upper jaw. Its skull is deeper and more square than those of its later relatives.

This 13-foot-long (4-meter) stegosaur also had a pair of shoulder spikes. *Huayangosaurus* is named for a village in China near where its remains were first discovered.

Huayangosaurus

KENTROSAURUS *(KEN-troh-sor-uss)*

shoulder spike from Kentrosaurus

The name *Kentrosaurus* means "pointed or spiked lizard." This dinosaur had several pairs of tall, slim plates along its neck and spine, but at the middle of the creature's back, the plates narrowed into sharp spikes. A pair of long spikes also stuck out sideways from the dinosaur's shoulders. A small stegosaur of the Late Jurassic Period, *Kentrosaurus* rarely grew to more than 16 feet (5 meters) in length, and it weighed about 4,000 pounds (1,800 kilograms).

Kentrosaurus

Lexovisaurus

LEXOVISAURUS *(leks-OH-vih-sor-uss)*

small, narrow head of Lexovisaurus

This Mid-Jurassic dinosaur is one of the earliest known stegosaurs. It measured about 18 feet (5.6 meters) long and seems to have had tall, thin plates and shoulder spikes. It was named for the Lexovians, an ancient group of people who once lived in the region of France where some of the dinosaur's remains were discovered.

Werner Janensch

WHERE ON EARTH?

Discovered in 1907 by Werner Janensch, the Tendaguru Beds (at Tendaguru Hill) are a rock formation in the Mtwara region of southeastern Tanzania in Africa. The dig site was difficult to reach and was plagued with biting flies, so animals weren't used to help carry fossils. Instead, over the first four years of digging, human porters carried out more than 500,000 pounds (225,000 kilograms) of material! The most interesting fossils recovered from Tendaguru included a huge *Brachiosaurus* and the first *Kentrosaurus*.

Why were the dinosaur bones there? Long ago, during the Late Jurassic Period, the area that formed Tendaguru was at the mouth of a river that emptied into a huge, shallow, muddy lagoon. Animals that died may have been washed into the lagoon, where a bank of sand prevented the bodies from being carried out to sea. Instead, they drifted to the bottom of the lagoon, only to be found millions of years later on a quiet, desolate hill many miles from the sea.

STEGOSAURUS *(steg-oh-SOR-uss)*

plate from over Stegosaurus's hip

Stegosaurus is one of the best known of all the dinosaurs. It was given its name, which means "plated or roofed lizard," because of the triangular plates that ran along its neck, back, and tail. The biggest of the plates—those located over the animal's hips—were as much as 3 feet (.95 meter) high and 3 feet (.95 meter) wide. At 25 feet (7.8 meters) in length and 11 feet (3.4 meters) in height at the hips, this creature was the largest of the stegosaurs. It probably weighed a hefty 8,000 pounds (3,600 kilograms).

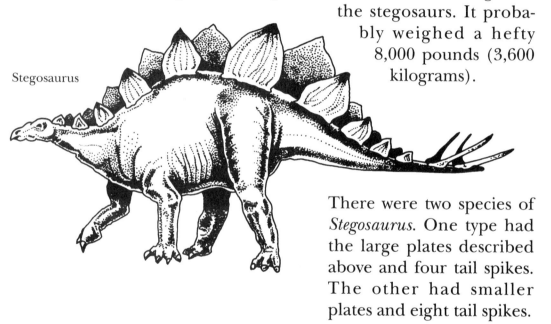

Stegosaurus

There were two species of *Stegosaurus*. One type had the large plates described above and four tail spikes. The other had smaller plates and eight tail spikes.

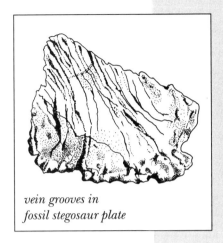

vein grooves in fossil stegosaur plate

STEGOSAUR PLATES

Some stegosaurs had large, flattened plates that may have acted as heat exchangers to help the dinosaur regulate its body temperature. Many fossil stegosaur plates are covered with webs of small grooves that may have been formed by tiny blood vessels under the skin's surface. This suggests that the dinosaur may have been able to turn its plates toward the sun to warm its blood, or away from the sun to allow cool breezes to cool it off. The plates also made the dinosaur look larger and more threatening to its foes, or perhaps more attractive to a possible mate.

WUERHOSAURUS *(woo-er-hoh-SOR-uss)*

hip plate of Wuerhosaurus

This dinosaur, named for the village in China near where it was found, caused some surprise when it was first discovered. It was among the stegosaurs found to have lived into the Cretaceous Period. The shape of this animal's flattened plates differed from those of its relatives. *Wuerhosaurus* was about 20 feet (6.2 meters) long and probably weighed 4,000 to 6,000 pounds (1,800 to 2,700 kilograms).

Wuerhosaurus

INVITE A STEGOSAUR TO YOUR PARTY!

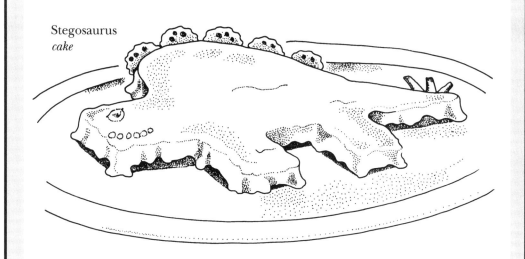

Stegosaurus *cake*

How would you like to feature a stegosaur as a special guest at your next birthday party? You won't be able to arrange a live appearance, but a stegosaur-shaped cake can be your party's star attraction. This *Stegosaurus* pattern is designed to be cut from a 14 x 11-inch (35.6 x 27.9-centimeter) sheet cake. Once the pieces are properly arranged on a platter and iced, you can add chocolate-chip cookie halves for stegosaur plates and gumdrops for eyes. For those party guests with a sweet tooth, this dinosaur is likely to be a real hit!

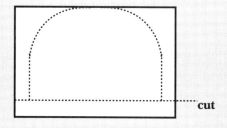

Cut Stegosaurus *pattern out of 14" x 11" (35.6 x 27.9 cm) sheet cake.*

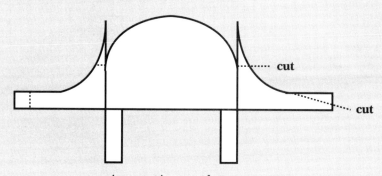

Arrange pieces on platter.

CHAPTER 7

DINOSAUR DIVERSITY

The Ornithopoda and the Pachycephalosauria

DINOSAUR HEADGEAR

Some of the crested, duckbilled dinosaurs had truly amazing headgear. But these terrific toppers were more than just decoration. A hollow-crested dinosaur may have used its crest to produce sound. The crest may also have improved the creature's sense of smell. Solid-crested dinosaurs may have used the crests to recognize others of their kind.

At one time, scientists grouped the Ornithopoda (or-nih-THOP-oh-duh) and Pachycephalosauria (pak-ee-sef-uh-loh-SOR-ee-uh) together, but that is no longer so. The ornithopods are a large suborder of the ornithischian group. These "bird-footed" dinosaurs were a hardy group, lasting from the Late Triassic Period through the end of the Cretaceous Period. In spite of their name, the feet of the ornithopods weren't very birdlike. Each hind foot had three or four toes that ended in rather stubby, hooflike claws. The creatures also had as many as five fingers on each hand.

Ornithopods (particularly the larger types) may have grazed leisurely on all fours, but they probably ran on their hind legs only, with their long tails held up and straight out for balance. Some of the ornithopods were small and almost lizardlike in appearance. Others were quite large and sported rather bizarre crests. However, they all had one trait in common: Like all ornithischians, they were plant-eaters.

The most obvious trait of the pachycephalosaur, or "dome-headed lizard," is its thickened skull. Some of these dinosaurs had high, rounded domes, some had flattened domes, and others even had

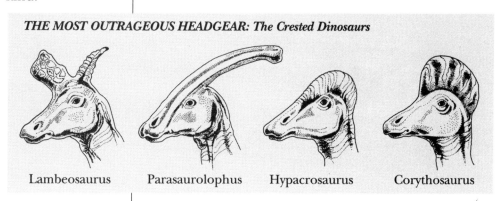

THE MOST OUTRAGEOUS HEADGEAR: The Crested Dinosaurs

Lambeosaurus   Parasaurolophus   Hypacrosaurus   Corythosaurus

divided domes. These creatures of the Late Cretaceous Period were bipedal plant-eaters with short, sharp teeth for clipping their food. Some pachycephalosaurs were as small as modern turkeys, while others reached lengths of 15 feet (4.7 meters).

HYPSILOPHODON *(hip-sih-LOF-oh-don)*

fossil Hypsilophodon *skull*

Hypsilophodon means "high-crested tooth." This animal is so named because of the high, ridged cheek teeth at the sides of its jaws. We know a lot about this dinosaur because some twenty excellent skeletons were found on the Isle of Wight in southern England.

For a Cretaceous dinosaur, *Hypsilophodon* had some primitive features. It had five fingers on its hands and four clawed toes on its feet. And although its snout ended in the shape of a narrow, flattened beak, it had teeth in the front of its jaws, unlike later ornithopods.

At first glance it seems that this small creature had few defenses. It was no more than 7 feet (2.2 meters) long and 2 feet (62 centimeters) tall, and it weighed only 140 pounds (63 kilograms). Nevertheless, it was among the swiftest of the early ornithopods and its ability to make a quick getaway helped it to avoid becoming a meal for a hungry predator.

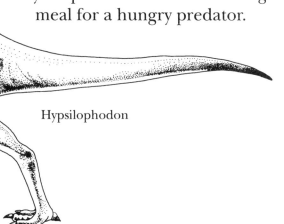

Hypsilophodon

IGUANODON *(ee-GWAN-oh-don)*

thumb spike on
Iguanodon*'s*
right hand

Iguanodon's modern claim to fame is that it was the first plant-eating dinosaur discovered and recognized as a whole new type of animal. It was up to 25 feet (7.8 meters) long and 15 feet (4.7 meters) high, and it weighed as much as 10,000 pounds (4,500 kilograms). Size alone may have been a good defense for this Early Cretaceous animal, but it also had sturdy thumb spikes that it may have used for protection. *Iguanodon* traveled in herds, and the remains of this dinosaur and its relatives have been found on every continent except Antarctica. *Iguanodon* was named because its teeth were (barely) similar to those of a modern iguana.

Iguanodon

EDMONTOSAURUS *(ed-MON-toh-sor-uss)*

distinctive pattern of
Edmontosaurus*'s skin*

This "duck lizard" belonged to a large group of ornithopods called duckbilled dinosaurs because of their wide, flat snouts. It was about 30 feet (9.3 meters) long, but it was slender for its size and weighed in at about 6,000 to 8,000 pounds (2,700 to 3,600 kilograms).

Fossilized impressions of *Edmontosaurus* suggest that its skin had a bumpy texture. It had a wide, flat, toothless snout and cheek teeth at the sides of its jaws, typical of other duckbills. With as many as one thousand cheek teeth arranged in tightly packed rows, this dinosaur was able to efficiently grind up its diet of pine needles, cones, seeds, and fruit. Worn or lost teeth were constantly replaced.

Edmontosaurus

HOW DO WE KNOW THAT SOME DINOSAURS TRAVELED IN HERDS?

One hint that dinosaurs traveled in herds is the discovery of large groups of fossil animals of the same kind in one area. In 1878, more than thirty adult *Iguanodons* were discovered together in a Belgian coal mine that had once been a ravine during the Mesozoic Era. It's possible that the entire group died together in a flood. Some scientists point out that the dinosaurs may have died at different times and then all been washed into the same resting place, giving the impression that they had died together. Still, a number of fossilized track-ways support the theory that *Iguanodon* moved in herds.

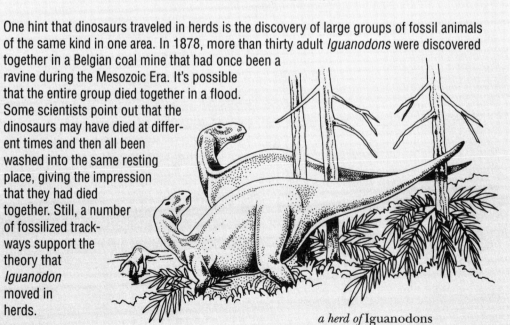

a herd of Iguanodons

DISCOVERIES

Type of dinosaur and the modern name of the country in which it was found

HYPSILOPHODON
• England (Wealden Marls, on the Isle of Wight)
• Spain (in the Las Zabacheras Beds, in the province of Teruel)

IGUANODON
• England (Wealden, in the counties of West Sussex, East Sussex, Surrey, and Kent, and the Isle of Wight)
• Belgium (Wealden, in the province of Hainaut)
• Spain (in the Las Zabacheras Beds, in the province of Teruel)
• Germany (Wealden, in the state of North Rhine-Westphalia)
• United States (in the Lakota Formation, in South Dakota)

EDMONTOSAURUS
• United States (in the Hell Creek Formation, in Montana and South Dakota, and in the Lance Formation, in Wyoming)

MAIASAURA
• United States (in the Upper Two Medicine Formation, in Montana)

LAMBEOSAURUS
• Canada (in the Judith River Formation, in Alberta)

PARASAUROLOPHUS
• Canada (in the Judith River Formation, in Alberta)
• United States (in the Kirtland Shale and the Fruitland Formation, in New Mexico)

PACHYCEPHALOSAURUS
• United States (in the Lance Formation, in Wyoming, and in the Hell Creek Formation, in South Dakota and Montana)

MAIASAURA *(my-ee-uh-SOR-uh)*

Maiasaura's
duckbill snout

Maiasaura, or "good mother lizard," lived during the Late Cretaceous Period. This creature earned its name because its remains were first discovered near a nest of fifteen baby dinosaurs. *Maiasaura* was about 30 feet (9.3 meters) long and 15 feet (4.7 meters) tall, and it weighed about 4,000 pounds (1,800 kilograms). It had the low head and wide, flat snout of a duckbill, and it sported a small, bony crest between its eyes.

Maiasaura

LAMBEOSAURUS
(lam-bee-oh-SOR-uss)

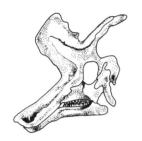

hollow-boned crest on Lambeosaurus *fossil skull*

Named in honor of paleontologist Lawrence Lambe, *Lambeosaurus* is the largest ornithischian ever found. It was usually about 30 feet (9.3 meters) in length, although one creature whose remains were discovered in Baja California may have been nearly 55 feet (17.1 meters) long. This Late Cretaceous duckbill dinosaur's most remarkable features included an odd, hatchet-shaped crest of hollow bone and a backward-pointing solid spike on its head. Some scientists suggest that *Lambeosaurus* may have used the crest to produce loud bellowing or hooting calls to threaten a rival, advertise for a mate, or warn a herdmate of danger.

JOHN HORNER

In 1978, paleontologist John Horner walked into a rock shop in Montana to look through the fossils that were offered for sale. He didn't find anything of particular interest until the owner brought out a coffee can that held a few very small bones. Horner and his associate, Bob Makela, immediately recognized the bones as those of a hatchling dinosaur and quickly asked permission to dig at the site where the fossils had been uncovered.

It didn't take long for them to discover a 6-foot-wide, 3-foot-deep (1.9-meter-wide, .95-meter-deep), bowl-shaped hole that had served as a dinosaur nest many millions of years ago. Within the nest were fifteen baby dinosaurs. The remains of an adult were found nearby.

This dinosaur was a new type. Since it seemed obvious from the worn condition of the babies' teeth that the adult had been feeding them while they were still in the nest, Horner named it *Maiasaura*, or "good mother lizard." Since then, hundreds of hatchlings, eggs, eggshells, nests, and even several adults have been found on the site now known as "Egg Mountain."

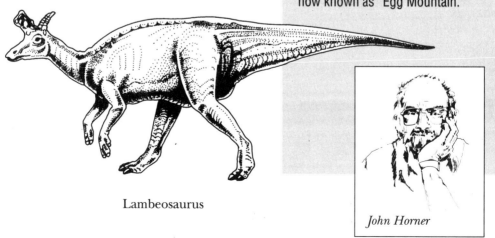

Lambeosaurus

John Horner

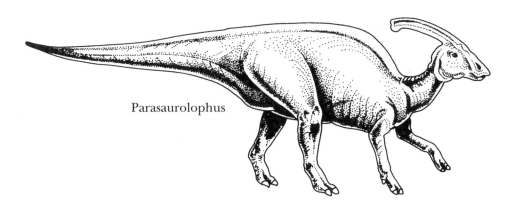

Parasaurolophus

PARASAUROLOPHUS *(par-uh-sor-ALL-oh-fuss)*

Parasaurolophus
fossil skull with crest

Although its name means "similar-crested lizard," *Parasaurolophus*'s crest truly stands out. The crest was hollow, and it arched backward from this Cretaceous duckbill's snout for 4 to 6 feet (1.2 to 1.9 meters). Inside the crest, a pair of nasal passages swept back from the nostrils, then curved forward again into the snout. This arrangement probably enabled the animal to trumpet loudly as it moved through the trees. A plant-eater with a spoon-shaped beak, this dinosaur ate pine needles and the leaves of primitive flowering trees.

Parasaurolophus was about 30 feet (9.3 meters) long and weighed between 6,000 and 10,000 pounds (2,700 to 4,500 kilograms). It also had a noticeably thick tail that may have been brightly colored or patterned.

PACHYCEPHALOSAURUS (pak-ee-sef-uh-loh-SOR-uss)

Pachycephalosaurus's "crash helmet"

This creature, which was 15 feet (4.7 meters) long, was the largest member of the suborder Pachycephalosauria. The top of its skull formed a huge, 10-inch-thick (25.4-centimeter) dome of solid bone, which was fringed with clusters of small, bony knobs. *Pachycephalosaurus*, or "thick-headed lizard," probably used its special "crash helmet" in a manner similar to that of modern rams. Rival males may have butted heads to win mates or to become the leader of the herd.

Pachycephalosaurus

THE FIRST DINOSAUR DISCOVERIES

Iguanodon *tooth fossil*

A British doctor, Gideon Mantell, is credited with discovering the first dinosaur remains to be recognized as evidence of a new life form. The legend is that in 1822, Dr. Mantell's wife found a strange tooth while taking a stroll and brought it home to her husband. A colleague noticed a similarity between the fossil tooth and the teeth of a South American iguana. Mantell was able to convince others of the importance of the tooth, and the new creature was dubbed *Iguanodon*.

Megalosaurus *tooth fossil*

In 1824, some teeth, ribs, and other bones were unearthed in England by a scientist named William Buckland. These remains were the first fossils publicly recognized as being those of a new kind of creature—a fierce meat-eater that came to be called *Megalosaurus*.

Hadrosaurus was described in 1858 by Joseph Leidy, a professor of anatomy. It was the first dinosaur discovered and identified in North America. By the end of the century, however, more than one hundred North American dinosaurs would be known.

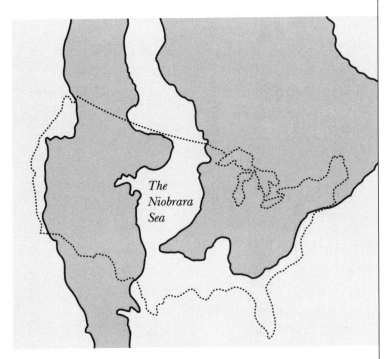

For much of the Mesozoic Era, the North American Midwest was underwater! During the Late Cretaceous Period, a shallow sea that was 1,000 miles (1,610 kilometers) wide stretched from the Arctic Ocean to the Gulf of Mexico. Among the creatures that swam in the warm waters of this huge sea were giant turtles as long as rowboats, and giant swimming reptiles known as the plesiosaurs.

DINOSAUR NEIGHBORS: THE PLESIOSAURS

The largest group of seagoing reptiles belonged to an order called *Plesiosauria* (plee-zee-oh-SOR-ee-uh), or "near lizards." These creatures are the models for fabled beasts such as Nessie, the legendary Loch Ness monster. Nessie is likely nothing more than the product of overactive imaginations, but the plesiosaurs really did exist, swimming gracefully through the warm waters of Mesozoic seas and feeding on fish or other reptiles.

Members of the order were divided into two groups, based on whether they had short necks or long necks. *Elasmosaurus* (ee-LAZ-moh-sor-uss), or "thin-plated lizard," was a long-necked plesiosaur.

In fact, its flexible neck accounted for nearly half of the animal's 45-foot (14-meter) length. *Elasmosaurus* probably swam slowly at the surface, with its neck arched high out of the water. When it spotted its prey, it would fling its head forward and strike, grasping its victim with sharply pointed teeth.

Kronosaurus (KROH-noh-sor-uss), named for Kronos, the Greek god of time, was the largest of the short-necked plesiosaurs. It measured 42 feet (13 meters) from nose to tail, and one-quarter of that length was in its massive skull. With its terrifying, 8-foot-long (2.5-meter), dagger-toothed jaws, this giant could swallow small prey whole or rip apart very large prey.

Elasmosaurus

Kronosaurus

CHAPTER 8

AMAZING ARMOR

The Ankylosaurs

The *Ankylosauria* (an-ky-loh-SOR-ee-uh), a suborder of the ornithischian group of dinosaurs, are often called armored tanks on four legs. There were two kinds of ankylosaurs, or "stiffened lizards," that lived during the Cretaceous Period. The first, the nodosaurids, were covered by a network of bony plates set into the tough skin on their neck, back, sides, and tail. Spikes lined the animal's sides for extra protection against predators. The later group, the ankylosaurids, also had body armor, but they either had no side spikes or small ones. Instead, they were equipped with a bony tail club that could probably knock over an animal the size of a modern elephant. Both types of ankylosaurs had flattened heads that usually ended in tough, toothless beaks that were useful for clipping plants.

The remains of these well-protected plant-eaters have been found on every continent, including Antarctica. A nest of six wolf-sized baby ankylosaurs was uncovered in the Gobi Desert in 1988. Five were huddled close together and another was, in one scientist's words, "curled up like a sleeping dog."

EDMONTONIA *(ed-mon-TOH-nee-uh)*

spike from over shoulder of Edmontonia

This "armored lizard" was one of the largest nodosaurs. It was about 20 feet (6.2 meters) long and weighed 6,000 to 8,000 pounds (2,700 to 3,600 kilograms). Broad, ridged plates protected its neck and shoulders, and smaller, bony studs covered its

---

DISCOVERIES

Type of dinosaur and the modern name of the country in which it was found

EDMONTONIA

• United States (in the Judith River Formation, in Montana, and in the Lance Formation, in Wyoming)

• Canada (in the Judith River Formation, the Horseshoe Canyon Formation, and the St. Mary River Formation, in Alberta)

EUOPLOCEPHALUS

• Canada (in the Judith River Formation, in Alberta)

• United States (in the Judith River Formation, in Montana)

NODOSAURUS

• United States (in the Mowry Shale, in Wyoming)

ANKYLOSAURUS

• United States (in the Hell Creek Formation, in Montana, and the Lance Formation, in Wyoming)

• Canada (in the Scollard Formation, in Alberta)

STRUTHIOSAURUS

• Romania (in the Sinpetru Beds, near Hunedoara)

• Austria (in the Gosau Formation, Niederöstereich)

Edmontonia

back, sides, and tail. Although *Edmontonia* had no tail club, this Late Cretaceous dinosaur probably defended itself quite well against predators. Some scientists think it might have charged attackers in the same way a rhinoceros would today. The animal's narrow head and snout were good for rooting around in ground-growing plants.

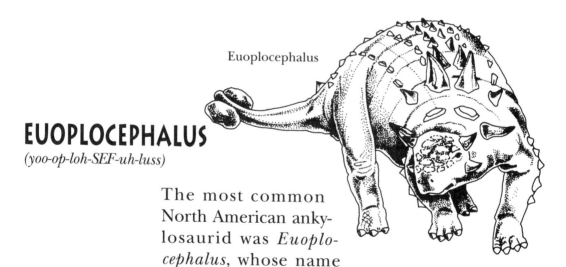

Euoplocephalus

EUOPLOCEPHALUS
(yoo-op-loh-SEF-uh-luss)

The most common North American ankylosaurid was *Euoplocephalus*, whose name means "well-armored head." This dinosaur was about 25 feet (7.8 meters) long and 8 feet (2.5 meters) wide, and its tail club measured nearly 3 feet (.95 meter) across. "Well armored" would have described not only this dinosaur's head, but its entire body as well. It was covered with bony plates that were small but tough, and its back was lined with large, bony studs and horny spikes. Its wide, triangular-shaped head ended in a horny

fossil Euoplocephalus *skull*

76

beak that may have been used to slice through leaves and twigs. *Euoplocephalus* probably browsed on any type of plant life that grew near the ground.

Nodosaurus

NODOSAURUS *(noh-doh-SOR-uss)*

Nodosaurus's bony knobs

One look at *Nodosaurus* is enough to explain why it was called "knobby lizard." This Early Cretaceous dinosaur's body was covered with a shield of bony knobs, plates, and studs. Although *Nodosaurus* lacked a tail club, it was sturdily built. This dinosaur, which was about 18 feet (5.6 meters) in length, had strong, powerful legs and broad feet to support its 6,000 pounds (2,700 kilograms) of bulk. The only thing that wasn't very big about this dinosaur was its head, which was long and slender. Its snout may have ended in the typical toothless ankylosaur beak, which was well suited for cutting vegetation. Like other nodosaurids, *Nodosaurus* also had tiny, weak, leaf-shaped teeth further back on its jaws.

WHERE DOES THE WORD *DINOSAUR* COME FROM?

Dinosaur remains were first recognized as being those of a new order of animal during the early 1800s. The newly discovered creatures were thought to be huge and lizardlike. In 1841, British scientist Dr. Richard Owen made up the word *dinosaur* from two Greek words, *deinos* and *sauros*, meaning "terrible" and "lizard."

ANKYLOSAURUS *(an-KY-loh-sor-uss)*

fossil of Ankylosaurus*'s tail club bone*

Ankylosaurus, or "stiffened lizard," was the largest and among the last of the ankylosaurs. At about 33 feet (10.2 meters) long and 6 feet (1.9 meters) wide, this ankylosaurid was built low and wide. It was studded from head to tail with rows of bony plates and knobs that were set into its leathery skin. This dinosaur was also equipped with tough, curved, hooflike claws on its feet. When attacked by a predator, this animal's most effective weapon was a huge double knob of bone at the end of its tail. When in danger, *Ankylosaurus* could swing this club, knocking an enemy off its feet or even breaking its leg.

Ankylosaurus

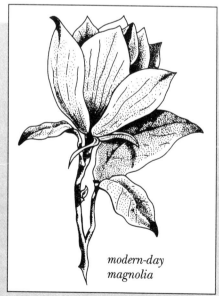

modern-day magnolia

THE FIRST FLOWERS

Flowers are usually far too delicate to form fossils. However, enough evidence exists to show that flowering plants first developed about 110 million years ago, during the Cretaceous Period.

Amazingly, in 1981 in Sweden, nearly perfect fossils were found of the tiny flowers of a plant called scania. Other evidence includes fossilized pollen, seedpods, and leaves. The oldest known fossil leaf from a flowering plant is one that is strikingly similar to a modern magnolia.

Once flowering plants had developed, they spread quickly. Today, more than 80 percent of plant life on Earth belongs to the flowering plant group.

STRUTHIOSAURUS *(strooth-ee-oh-SOR-uss)*

spike on
Struthiosaurus*'s back*

Not all ankylosaurs were large. *Struthiosaurus*, or "harsh lizard," was likely no more than 6 feet (1.9 meters) long and probably weighed about 2,000 pounds (900 kilograms). Although it was small, this nodosaurid had a suit of armor, like its larger relatives. The one exception, however, was that its head was unarmed.

Struthiosaurus roamed on what were then islands in the sea that once covered much of Europe during Late Cretaceous times. Its remains have been found in what are now Austria and Romania.

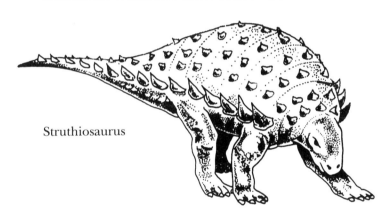

Struthiosaurus

RECORD HOLDER: THE WORLD'S LARGEST CROCODILE

Deinosuchus (dy-noh-SOOK-uss) is the largest known member of the crocodile group. Scientists calculate that this creature may have been more than 50 feet (15.5 meters) long. Its name means "terrible crocodile." A fossilized skull of a *Deinosuchus* was discovered in the remains of a former Late Cretaceous swamp in Texas, and other fossils of this ancient crocodile have been discovered in Montana and Mississippi.

Deinosuchus

DINOSAUR NEIGHBORS: THE FIRST SNAKES

Pachyrhachis

Snakes first appeared early in the Cretaceous Period. They probably developed from burrowing lizards, or perhaps from a seagoing lizard such as *Pachyrhachis* (pak-ee-RAH-kiss). Modern boas and pythons have the tiny remains of a hipbone, which suggests that their ancestors had legs. The oldest fossil serpents are most closely related to the modern snake family that includes constrictors (snakes that tighten around prey animals so that they can't breathe). Found in Argentina, *Dinilysia* (dy-nee-LEE-zee-uh), or "terrible destroyer," was probably a constrictor. This creature fed on small mammals, lizards, insects, and maybe even young dinosaurs.

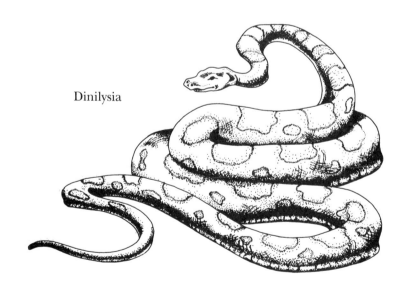

Dinilysia

CHAPTER 9

HORNS AND FRILLS
The Ceratopsians

The ceratopsians (sayr-uh-TOP-see-unz) were the last of the bird-hipped ornithischians to develop during the Cretaceous Period. As a group, they didn't survive as long as many other types of dinosaur groups, but they were otherwise very successful. In the 20 million years of their existence, they spread throughout what is now North America and Asia in great numbers.

These animals generally had a bony neck frill, and their jaws ended in a parrotlike "beak." The earliest ceratopsians walked mainly on two legs, and their frills were barely visible. Later ceratopsians were four-legged animals that developed larger and more unusual frills, as well as impressive horns. All ceratopsians were plant-eaters.

PSITTACOSAURUS *(sit-uh-coh-SOR-uss)*

Psittacosaurus, or "parrot lizard," represents a very early group of dinosaurs that shared characteristics with both ornithopods and ceratopsians. This 8-foot-long (2.5-meter) dinosaur did not have horns or an obvious neck frill, but it did have a short, backward-pointing spine at the edge of its skull. And although *Psittacosaurus* was not a direct ancestor of the horned dinosaurs that would develop

Psittacosaurus

HOW OLD COULD A DINOSAUR LIVE TO BE?

The life span was probably different for each dinosaur group. There is fossil evidence that certain large dinosaurs reached ages of 120 years or possibly more. Scientists also suggest that many species didn't stop growing at a particular age, but continued to grow very slowly throughout their adult lives.

fossil of Psittacosaurus*'s beaked skull*

later in the Cretaceous Period, it possessed a similar sharp, bony beak. This dinosaur often raised itself up from its short arms and narrow, clawed hands to walk upright.

PROTOCERATOPS
(proh-toh-SAYR-uh-tops)

Protoceratops was an early horned dinosaur. Despite its name, which means "first horned face," it had no horns on its face (although males may have had a slight bony rise above the beak). It did, however, have a sturdy, bony neck frill. This four-legged plant-eater cut the leaves and twigs of low-growing plants with its parrotlike beak, then sliced the food to pieces with rows of shearing teeth. *Protoceratops* was about 6 to 9 feet (1.9 to 2.8 meters) long and weighed around 400 pounds (180 kilograms).

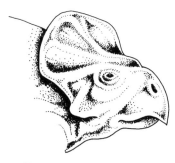

Protoceratops's *neck frill*

DISCOVERIES

Type of dinosaur and the modern name of the country in which it was found

PSITTACOSAURUS
• China (in the Lisangou Formation and the Xinpongnaobao Formation, in Inner Mongolia; in the Quingshan Formation in the province of Shandong; and in the Lianmugin Formation, in the province of Xinjiang Uygur Zizhiqu)
• Mongolia (many locations in Dundgov)

PROTOCERATOPS
• Mongolia (in the Djadochta Formation, Beds of Toogreeg, in Omnogov)
• China (in the Minhe Formation, in the province of Nei Mongol Zizhiqu)

BAGACERATOPS
• Mongolia (in the Red Beds of Khermeen Tsav, in Omnogov)

STYRACOSAURUS
• Canada (in the Judith River Formation, in Alberta)
• United States (in the Two Medicine Formation, in Montana)

TRICERATOPS
• United States (in the Lance Formation and the Evanston Formation, in Wyoming; the Hell Creek Formation, in Montana and South Dakota; and the Laramie Formation, in Colorado)
• Canada (in the Scollard Formation, in Alberta, and the Frenchman Formation, in Saskatchewan)

CHASMOSAURUS
• Canada (in the Judith River Formation, in Alberta)
• United States (in the Aguja Formation, in Texas, and in the Judith River Formation, in Montana)

TOROSAURUS
• United States (in the Lance Formation, in Wyoming; the Hell Creek Formation, in Montana and South Dakota; the North Horn Formation, in Utah; and the Javelina Formation, in Texas)
• Canada (in the Frenchman Formation, in Saskatchewan)

Protoceratops

ROY CHAPMAN ANDREWS

Roy Chapman Andrews

In April of 1922, explorer and naturalist Roy Chapman Andrews set out into the Gobi Desert in Asia to search for the bones of our human ancestors. Under his direction, forty men battled scorching heat, choking dust storms, and bandits to uncover what would be a most startling discovery. In an area called Flaming Cliffs, they found the remains of a new type of dinosaur. They called it *Protoceratops andrewsi*, in honor of Andrews.

On July 13 of the following year, Andrews and his companions discovered fossil dinosaur eggs. The 8-inch-long (20.3-centimeter), oval-shaped eggs (thought to be those of a *Protoceratops*) were in a large pit scooped from the red sand. They rested in a spiral pattern, which suggests that the mother either moved around the nest as she laid her eggs or positioned them after they had been laid. Before the eggs could hatch, the nest was buried by a sandstorm. Paleontologists had long suspected that dinosaurs had laid eggs, like other reptiles, but now they had positive proof.

Andrews visited the Gobi Desert on five separate expeditions. During that time, he and his associates uncovered other new dinosaur species, including *Velociraptor*, *Oviraptor*, *Pinacosaurus* (an armored dinosaur), and *Saurornithoides*. The tiny skull of a Cretaceous mammal was also found.

Roy Chapman Andrews discovered a nest of Protoceratops *eggs in the Gobi Desert.*

BAGACERATOPS *(bag-uh-SAYR-uh-tops)*

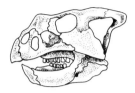

fossil Bagaceratops *skull*

This dinosaur's name means "small horned face," and the title certainly fits. Overall, the little creature was only about 3 feet (.95 meter) long. An early member of the ceratopsian group, *Bagaceratops* belonged to a family known as the protoceratopsids, or "before horned face." This dinosaur, however, did have a short, bony ridge along the back of its skull that looked like a miniature frill, and a small, stubby horn on its snout. It also had another advanced feature that would be common in later ceratopsians: It had no teeth in its curved upper beak.

Bagaceratops

STYRACOSAURUS *(sty-RAK-uh-sor-uss)*

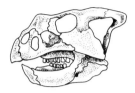

pointed frill on Styracosaurus*'s skull*

Styracosaurus was a short-frilled ceratopsian that was about 17 feet (5.3 meters) long and weighed about 8,000 pounds (3,600 kilograms). Many small points lined the sides of its frill, and there were six huge spikes along the frill's back arch. *Styracosaurus*, or "spiked lizard," had an impressive 2½-foot-long (78-centimeter) nose horn above its down-turned beak. As with most short-frilled ceratopsians, this dinosaur had openings in its frill that lightened it. Nevertheless, the animal was very powerfully built around the shoulders to enable it to support and move its massive head.

Styracosaurus

TRICERATOPS *(try-SAYR-uh-tops)*

Triceratops was as tall as an elephant and just as sturdily built. It stood about 9 feet (2.8 meters) high at the shoulder, was nearly 30 feet (9.3 meters) in length, and weighed between 20,000 and 24,000 pounds (9,000 and 10,800 kilograms). It also had an incredibly large head—one fossil skull measured 7 feet (2.2 meters) long! This dinosaur's head, which made up nearly one-quarter of the animal's total length, probably weighed more than 2,000 pounds (900 kilograms)! The back of the skull extended out to form a solid, bony frill lined with bony knobs along the edge.

Triceratops's brow horn

Triceratops

The animal's long snout ended in a curved, horn-covered beak designed for clipping tough branches and for shearing off leaves and twigs. *Triceratops* used its strong cheek teeth to slice vegetation into smaller pieces. This dinosaur, whose name means "three-horned face," also sported three horns on its head. The nose horn was thick and stubby, but the two brow horns were as long as 4 feet (1.2 meters) each.

CHASMOSAURUS *(KAZ-moh-sor-uss)*

frill bone openings on fossil Chasmosaurus *skull*

Chasmosaurus was one of the first long-frilled, horned dinosaurs. Large, skin-covered openings in the creature's spiked frill inspired its name, which means "opening lizard." Without these openings, the animal's huge frill would have been too heavy for it to lift. Scientists believe that the dinosaur's powerful jaw muscles were anchored to the frill, giving the animal a very strong bite. The frill was probably also used to intimidate rivals and predators or to attract a mate. This 16-foot-long (5-meter), 5,000-pound (2,250-kilogram) ceratopsian had two long, curved horns over its eyes and a shorter horn on its snout.

Chasmosaurus

TOROSAURUS *(tor-oh-SOR-uss)*

nose horn of
Torosaurus

Torosaurus, or "piercing lizard," had the longest frill of any ceratopsian—nearly 5½ feet (1.7 meters) long. The creature's skull, measured from the tip of its beak to the back of its frill, was almost 9 feet (2.8 meters) in length! The frill extended well over *Torosaurus*'s shoulder area, so it probably helped to protect the back of the dinosaur's neck from attack. A short nose horn and a pair of brow horns added to the animal's defenses, but at 20 feet (6.2 meters) long and nearly 10,000 pounds (4,500 kilograms) in weight, *Torosaurus* was a match for most predators.

Torosaurus

RECORD-SETTING HORNS AND FRILLS

Torosaurus	longest frill	5½ feet (1.7 meters)
Styracosaurus	most frill spikes	6
	longest nose horn	2½ feet (77 centimeters)
Triceratops	longest brow horn	4 feet (1.2 meters)

HOW BIG WERE DINOSAUR EGGS?

The size of the eggs varied depending on the type of dinosaur, but even for the giant dinosaurs, jumbo eggs wouldn't have worked. The shell of a giant egg would have been too thick for a hatchling to break through.

Until recently, the largest egg known belonged to a sauropod, probably the 40-foot-long (12.4-meter) *Hypselosaurus*. The baby dinosaur that hatched from that soccer-ball-sized egg would have weighed about 2 pounds (.9 kilogram), but it would have grown to weigh 20,000 pounds (9,000 kilograms) as an adult!

Other eggs have now been discovered in China that are 16 to 18 inches (40.6 to 45.7 centimeters) long and 6 to 8 inches (15.2 to 20.3 centimeters) wide. The type of dinosaur that laid the eggs is still unknown.

chicken egg

sauropod egg

PART IV: THE FINAL ACT

The End of the Dinosaurs

About 65 million years ago, something happened that destroyed almost 75 percent of the animals living at that time. The dinosaurs disappeared, and the Mesozoic Era came to an end.

Paleontologists have proposed several theories to explain why the dinosaurs died. Two theories, however, seem to lead the pack. The first is that dinosaurs were not able to adjust well enough to the changes in climate and in the environment that were brought on by a drop in sea level. The second theory is that a collision between Earth and an asteroid caused incredible and immediate changes on Earth, changes that the dinosaurs could not survive. After the crash,

Some scientists believe that an asteroid colliding with Earth may have brought about the end of the dinosaurs.

WHAT DOES EXTINCTION MEAN?

Extinction is the end of existence for an entire group of living things. One scientist calculated that 99 percent of all living things that have ever developed on Earth have become extinct!

enough dust would have been thrown into the air to blot out the sunlight for months. Also, the fireball that would have occurred on impact might have set off forest fires that raced across the land, adding even more smoke and soot to the already blackened sky. Much of the tiny plantlike plankton that floated on the surface of the sea would have been destroyed, along with many land plants. There would have been little food left. The Earth would have become a cold, dark place. Smaller animals may have been able to survive, but for the dinosaurs, it was the end.

Many paleontologists believe that the end of the dinosaur age was a result of a combinaton of these and other factors. What do you think?

Although many types of creatures died at the end of the Mesozoic Era, others survived. Here are a few examples of each:

THE CASUALTIES	THE SURVIVORS
Ammonites (shellfish)	Sharks and Bony Fish
Dinosaurs	Crocodiles
Ichthyosaurs (sea reptiles)	Snakes
Mosasaurs (sea reptiles)	Gastropods (snails)
Pterosaurs	Lizards
Plesiosaurs	Mammals Birds Turtles

PERIODS OF EXTINCTION

The Mesozoic Era began after a severe period of extinction brought an end to the Paleozoic Era, or the time of "old life." Other extinctions followed, then the Mesozoic Era ended with another major extinction—one that spelled doom for the dinosaurs. This extinction marked the beginning of the Cenozoic Era, or the time of "new life." Extinctions do not necessarily take place all at once, but in waves of crisis called "events."

Era	Period (Millions of Years Ago)	Approximate Periods of Extinction (Millions of Years Ago) and Victims
Mesozoic	Cretaceous (144–65)	**65** dinosaurs ichthyosaurs pterosaurs plesiosaurs *Tyrannosaurus rex*
Mesozoic	Jurassic (208–144)	**144** many bivalves many ammonoids some marine reptiles many stegosaurs many sauropods *Stegosaurus*
Mesozoic	Triassic (245–208)	**213** most remaining therapsids placodonts thecodonts (dinosaur ancestors) many brachiopods many gastropods *Ornithosuchus*
Paleozoic	Permian (286–245)	**245** many soft corals many brachiopods bryozoans many ammonoids many therapsids (mammal-like reptiles) *Lycaenops*

WHAT'S IN A NAME?

The scientific names that are given to living or once living things (including dinosaurs) are a sort of international language that helps to avoid confusion in the identification of a plant or animal. These names are usually from Greek or Latin words.

This method was developed by an eighteenth-century Swedish botanist, Carl von Linne (also known as Carolus Linnaeus). He created a catalog of living things, giving each organism a Latin or Greek name that described something about it (for example, its physical characteristics, or the name of the area where it was found).

This practice was in wide use by the time the dinosaurs were discovered, so it was applied to them as well. Just hearing a dinosaur's name can often give you a hint of the type of creature it was. For example, *tri* means "three," and *cerato* means "horned." Knowing this, you can safely assume that *Triceratops* had three horns.

Try making up dinosaurlike names for your friends and family. Knowing the meaning of a few simple, commonly used Greek or Latin roots is the key. The root words listed below will give you a good start. A prefix is found at the beginning of a word. A suffix is found at the end of a word. For example, if you have a dog with long, fluffy ears and a short tail, you might call your pet *Dasyoto-microurus*. Give it a try!

PREFIX	LANGUAGE	PRONUN-CIATION	MEANING	PREFIX	LANGUAGE	PRONUN-CIATION	MEANING
a-	G	AH-ee	without	frigo-	L	FREE-goh	cold
abricto-	G	uh-BRIK-toh	wide awake	hetero-	G	HET-er-oh	different
aeto-	L	AY-toh	aged	hypsi-	G	HIP-see	high
alectro-	G	uh-LEK-troh	unmarried, alone	kentro-	G	KEN-troh	spiked
allo-	G	AL-oh	other	lepto-	G	LEP-toh	weak
alti-	L	AL-tee	high	mani-	L	MAHN-ee	hand
anato-	L	uh-NAT-oh	duck	megalo-	G	MEG-uh-loh	large
aniso-	G	uh-NEE-soh	unequal	micro-	G	MY-kroh	small
antarcto-	G	ant-ARK-toh	southern	mono-	G	MAHN-oh	one
antro-	G	AN-troh	cavern	nano-	G	NAN-oh	dwarf
apato-	G	uh-PAT-oh	deceptive	naso-	L	NAY-zoh	nose
aqua-	L	AH-kwuh	water	necto-	G	NEK-toh	swimming
archi-	G	AR-kee	primitive	neo-	G	NEE-oh	new
aristo-	G	uh-RIST-oh	best	noto-	G	NOH-toh	back
astro-	G	AS-troh	star	octo-	G	OK-toh	eight
atro-	L	AA-troh	black	omni-	G	OM-nee	all
auri-	L	OR-ee	ear	ophio-	G	OH-fee-oh	serpent
baro-	G	BAYR-oh	heavy	ornitho-	G	OR-nith-oh	bird
brachio-	G	BRAK-ee-oh	arm	osmo-	G	OZ-moh	smell
brachy-	G	BRAK-ee	short	oto-	G	OH-toh	ear
bronto-	G	BRON-toh	thunder	ovi-	L	OH-vee	egg
camara-	G	KAM-ah-ruh	chamber	pachy-	G	PAK-ee	thick
campto-	G	KAMP-toh	bent	patri-	G	PAH-tree	father
cerato-	G	sayr-AT-oh	horned	penta-	G	PEN-tuh	five
coel-	L	SEEL	hollow	phago-	G	FAY-joh	eating
compso-	G	COMP-soh	elegant	platy-	G	PLAT-ee	wide, flat
cory-	G	KOR-ee	helmet	plesio-	G	PLEE-zee-oh	near
dasy-	G	DAZ-ee	hairy	poly-	G	PAHL-ee	many
di-	G	DY	two	proto-	G	PROH-toh	first
dino-	G	DY-noh	terrible	pseudo	G	SOO-doh	false
diplo-	G	DIP-luh	double	ptero-	G	TAYR-oh	wing
dryo-	G	DRY-uh	oak	retro-	L	REH-troh	backward
ecto-	G	EK-toh	outside	rhodo-	G	ROH-doh	red
elaphro-	G	ee-LAF-roh	lightweight	salto-	L	SAL-toh	leaping
endo-	G	EN-doh	inside	sapro-	G	SAP-roh	rotten
erythro-	G	eh-REE-throh	red				

Continued on next page

PREFIX	LANGUAGE	PRONUN-CIATION	MEANING
sarco-	G	SAR-koh	flesh
saur-	G	SOR	lizard
sclero-	G	SKLAYR-oh	hard
spheno-	G	SFEE-noh	wedge-shaped
stego-	G	STEG-oh	roofed, plated
tecno-	G	TEK-noh	child
tenui-	L	TEN-wee	thin
tetra-	G	TEH-truh	four
thero-	G	THAYR-oh	beast
titano-	G	ty-TAN-oh	gigantic
tri-	G	TRY	three
tyranno-	G	ty-RAN-oh	tyrant
ultra-	L	UL-truh	beyond
veloci-	L	vuh-LOSS-ih	swift
xeno-	G	ZEE-noh	strange

SUFFIX	LANGUAGE	PRONUN-CIATION	MEANING
-cephalic	G	seh-FAL-ik	head
-dactyl	G	DAK-til	finger
-demus	G	DEE-muss	body
-docus	G	DOH-kuss	beam
-gnathus	G	NAY-thuss	jaw
-ichthys	G	IK-thiss	fish
-ischian	G	ISS-kee-an	hip joint
-lestes	G	LESS-teez	robber
-lophus	G	LOH-fuss	crested
-mimus	L	MY-muss	mimic
-nychus	G	NYK-uss	claw
-odon	G	oh-DON	tooth
-pod	L	PAHD	foot
-pteryx	G	TAYR-iks	wing
-raptor	L	RAP-tor	thief
-saurus	G	SOR-uss	lizard
-spinax	L	SPIN-aks	spine
-urus	G	UR-uss	tail
-venator	G	VEN-uh-tor	hunter

INDEX

(The page number of the main description of each dinosaur is in bold type.)

activities
    fossil fun 10
    stegosaur cake 64
    Tyrannosaurus mask 41
age 81
Alamosaurus 49, **53**
Albertosaurus **36**, 37
Allosaurus 16, 18, 37, **39**
ammonites 12, 90
Anchisaurus **42**
Andrews, Roy Chapman 83
ankylosaurs 58, 75
Ankylosaurus 58, 75, **78**
    teeth 38
Apatosaurus 7, 16, 17, 18, **49**, 51, 56
archosaurs 4, 15
bacteria 11
Bagaceratops 82, **84**
Baldwin, David 22
birds 34, 90
body temperature 29, 34, 40, 63
Brachiosaurus 49, **52**, 56, 61
    teeth 38
Brontosaurus
    see *Apatosaurus*
Buckland, William 72
Camarasaurus 18, 19, 49, **50**, 51, 52
    teeth 38
carnosaurs 35
ceratopsians 81
ceratosaurs 20
Ceratosaurus 18, 20, **21**
Chasmosaurus 82, **86**
Coelophysis 6, 15, 18, 20, **21**, 22, 25, 52
coelurosaurs 20
Colbert, Edwin Harris 22, 25
Compsognathus 20, 25, **26**
Cope, Edward Drinker 22, 52
Corythosaurus 65
crests 65
Cretaceous Period 8
deinonychosaurs 29
Deinonychus 18, **29**, 33
Deinosuchus 79
Dinilysia 80
Diplodocus 11, 49, 52, **53**, 56

Dolomedes 13
Dromaeosaurus 29, **32**
Edmontonia **75**
Edmontosaurus **67**, 69
Efrassia 42, **45**
Egg Mountain 70
eggs 14, 83, 88
Euoplocephalus 75, **76**
extinction 89, 90, 91
fossils 11, 12, 13
Frass, E. 45
Gallimimus 20, **23**, 24
gastroliths 53
geological time 5
Ghost Ranch 15, 22, 25
Gorgosaurus
    see *Albertosaurus*
Iguanodon 58, **67**, 68, 69, 72
    teeth 38
Hadrosaurus 72
Herrerasaurus 6, 48
Homeosaurus 12
Horner, John 70
Huayangosaurus **59**
Hypacrosaurus 65
Hypselosaurus
    eggs 14, 88
Hypsilophodon 58, **66**, 69
ichthyosaurs 11, 27, 90
    Ichthyosaurus 9
Janensch, Werner 61
Jensen, Jim 25
Jurassic Period 7
Kentrosaurus 59, **60**, 61
Lagosuchus 48
Lambeosaurus 65, 69, **70**
Leidy, Joseph 72
Lexovisaurus 59, **61**
Linnaeus, Carolus 92
Lystrosaurus 25
Maiasaura **69**, 70
    eggs 14
Makela, Bob 70
Mamenchisaurus 49, **55**
mammals 34, 46, 83, 90
Mantell, Gideon 72

Marsh, O. C. 51, 52
Massospondylus 42, **46**
Megalosaurus 16, 17, **37**, 72
Megazostrodon 47
Mesolimus 12
Mesozoic Era 5, 73
    climate 6, 7, 8
Meyer, Grant 30
Monoclonius 52
Monolophosaurus 16
Mononychus 34
Morrison Formation 57
mosasaurs 90
Mussaurus 42, **43**
Niobrara Sea 73
nodosaurids 75
Nodosaurus 75, **77**
ornithischians 16
    family tree 58
ornithomimosaurs 20
Ornithomimus 18, 20, **23**
ornithopods 58, 65
Orodromeus
    eggs 14
Ostrom, John 30, 34
Oviraptor 18, 20, **24**, 83
oviraptorosaurs 20
Owen, Richard 77
pachycephalosaurs 58, 65
Pachycephalosaurus 58, 69, **72**
Pachyrhachïs 80
Pangaea 5
Panthalassa 5
Parasaurolophus 65, 69, **71**
Pinacosaurus 83
plants 28
    algae 28
    conifers 6, 28
    Cooksonia 28
    cycads 7, 28
    flowering 8, 28, 78
    grass 28
    horsetail 28
    seed ferns 13
    tree ferns 6, 7, 28
Plateosaurus 18, 42, **44**
    teeth 38
plesiosaurs 11, 73, 90
    Elasmosaurus 12, 73
    Kronosaurus 9, 74
    Plesiosaurus 9

Procompsognathus 20, **25**
prosauropods 18, 42
Protoceratops 24, 30, **82**
    eggs 14, 83
Psittacosaurus **81**, 82
pterosaurs 4, 56, 90
    Pterodactylus 9, 57
    Quetzalcoatlus 57
    Rhamphorhynchus 9, 56
Riojasaurus 42, **44**
Saltasaurus 49, **54**
Saltopus 20, **26**
saurischians 16, 17
    family tree 19
sauropods 18, 49, 91
sauropodomorphs 17, 18, 42, 49
Saurornithoides 29, **31**, 83
Seismosaurus 56
Sinraptor 16
snakes 80, 90
speed 24
Spinosaurus 37, **40**
Staurikosaurus 48
stegosaurs 58, 59, 91
Stegosaurus 52, 58, 59, **62**, 91
Stenonychosaurus 33
Struthiomimus 20, **22**
Struthiosaurus 75, **79**
Styracosaurus 82, **84**, 87
Sundance Sea 57
Supersaurus 56
teeth 38
Tendaguru Beds 61
Tenontosaurus 33
thecodonts 91
therapsids 25, 91
theropods 17
Torosaurus 82, **87**
Triassic Period 6
Triceratops 52, 58, 82, **85**, 87, 92
Troödon 29, **32**
    teeth 38
Tyrannosaurus 8, 15, 16, 17, 18, **35**, 37, 91
    teeth 38
Velociraptor 29, **30,** 83
von Linne, Carl
    see Linnaeus, Carolus
weight 39
Whitaker, George 22
Wuerhosaurus 59, **63**